WEAVER'S DAUGHTER

Also by Kimberly Brubaker Bradley

RUTHIE'S GIFT
ONE-OF-A-KIND MALLIE

WEAVER'S DAUGHTER

Kimberly Brubaker Bradley

DELACORTE PRESS

Published by
Delacorte Press
an imprint of
Random House Children's Books
a division of Random House, Inc.
1540 Broadway
New York, New York 10036

Visit us on the Web! www.randomhouse.com/kids
Educators and librarians, for a variety of teaching tools, visit us at
www.randomhouse.com/teachers

Library of Congress Cataloging-in-Publication Data

Bradley, Kimberly Brubaker.
    Weaver's daughter / Kimberly Brubaker Bradley.
        p. cm.
    Summary: In 1791 after her family's journey from Pennsylvania, ten-year-old Lizzie suffers from the disease of asthma in her new home in the Southwest Territory (present-day Tennessee).
    ISBN 0-385-32769-2
    [1. Asthma—Fiction. 2. Frontier and pioneer life—Tennessee—Fiction. 3. Tennessee—History—Fiction.] I. Title.
PZ7.B7247 We 2000
[Fic]—dc21   00-026193

The text of this book is set in 13-point Bembo.
Book design by Trish P. Watts
Manufactured in the United States of America
October 2000
10 9 8 7 6 5 4 3 2 1
BVG

To my mother and father

PROLOGUE

I have always had a clear head. Like my older sister, Hezzy, I remember many things. Like my younger sister, Nan, I remember them true. Yet I scarce remember our trip overmountain. For 'twas during our long journey, as summer blended into fall, that I suffered my first truly bad spell of sickness. I was six years old at the time.

As we struggled onward, my chest grew heavier and heavier, tighter and tighter. I rode in the wagon while my sisters walked. Ma made a nest of quilts for me between the sacks of cornmeal and the hard wooden pieces of her loom; I slipped my hand among the sacks and clutched the side of the wagon to hold myself upright. I struggled to breathe. The wagon lurched and thudded. I held on, and breathed, and longed for the stillness of the end of the day.

At night Ma would prop me close to the fire so the smoke might clear my lungs. She would wipe my streaming nose and bathe my swollen eyes. She would make tea from her dried herbs and feed me, sip by sip.

That is what I remember of the journey overmountain.

Nan speaks of the trip with pride. Four years old, she walked almost the entire way, from our old farm in Pennsylvania to our new one in what is now called the Southwest Territory, the land just west of Virginia.

Nan does not remember much of our old home. Hezzy remembers. She and I sometimes talk of the farm we had in Pennsylvania. In truth, it much resembled the farm we have now, four years later—cabin, barn, fields, and garden. The cabin has a stone foundation here, because stones are plentiful. We have apple trees where before we had strawberries. We look out on mountains instead of a river. The air smells different. And we have prospered here, our farm is larger, our table full.

I am ten years old. Hezzy is twelve, Nan is eight. We have six sheep, and hope for more in the spring. Pa laughs often here. Ma's loom sounds the same.

CHAPTER ONE

"I can pick apples," I said. "I know a ripe one from a green one just as well as Hezzy and Nan."

Ma stopped weaving. The *clack-clack-thump* that had filled the cabin all morning stopped too.

"Better than Nan," I said.

Ma looked at me for a long minute. "Sit," she said. "You are just as useful inside."

"Yes, Ma." I squirmed. 'Twas autumn, and our old trees were filled with ripened fruit. I sliced an apple with Ma's knife and strung the slices on a string. I draped the strings above the hearth to dry. Piles of apples waited on the table in front of me. I could never keep up. 'Twas not fair. I should be picking, too, and then we could all slice and string.

Clack-clack-thump, clack-clack-thump, clack-clack-

thump. Ma was weaving a coverlet of indigo-blue and butternut-yellow wool. When she was finished she would take it to Jonesborough and trade it for a sow, a mother pig. Next spring we would have piglets, and after that we would be rich in ham and bacon and lard.

I smothered a cough against my hand. I looked at Ma to see if she noticed. She did not. Her hands worked the loom steadily. *Clack-clack-thump*. I wished to be a weaver someday. Already I could weave plain cloth, and I spun better than both Nan and Hezzy. Nan did not have a mind for such things. Hezzy wove fancywork, near as well as Ma.

A bird chirruped outside the open door. A red leaf blew into the cabin and lay against my foot. I kept my hands steady to their task but could not keep my mind so well occupied. It was autumn. My sickness time. And I felt the sickness coming.

An apple rolled to the floor. I picked it up and bit into it. Its spicy sweetness filled my mouth. Our trees, neglected as they were before we came, still yielded good fruit.

I looked about the cabin. Ma's loom, the bed and the underbed beneath it took up one whole side. Besides, we had a spinning wheel, table, two benches, even a ladder-back chair. Pa had built shelves on either side of the hearth to hold our cooking gear, and the half-loft above the loom and bed would soon be filled with the fruits of our harvest. Including the apples I was stringing.

Clack-clack-thump, clack-clack-thump. I had awoken that morning with a tightness in my chest and a heaviness through my nose. Winter, spring, summer, all the year past, I had prayed every day like Jesus in the garden that this be taken from me.

Clack-clack-thump.

Suddenly I coughed hard. *Clack.* Ma's hands went still. The loom stopped. Ma looked to me. "'Tis nothing," I said. "Nothing." We both knew why Ma had kept me indoors today, but neither of us would say it.

Hezzy burst through the doorway with a basket of apples. "That's three of mine now to Nan's one," she said, upending the basket onto the table. Apples rolled everywhere. Some fell to the floor.

Ma and I looked at Hezzy. Slowly Ma smiled. "Aye, then, what has Nan found?" she asked. She thumped the beater onto her weaving and started the shuttle again. *Clack-clack-thump, clack-clack-thump.*

Hezzy grinned. "Nothing but an old worm. She's watching it walk up a stick."

I cut an apple and handed half to Hezzy. She ate it, smiling. I smiled back. Nan paid attention to small things. Hezzy was the one to climb among the tree's highest branches, Nan the one to sit and peer at a stick.

My friend Suzy Pearlette said I was exactly in the middle of my sisters: halfway like Nan, halfway like Hezzy. But today I was neither on the ground nor in the tree. I was the one to sit in the cabin, to not pick apples at all.

"Tell your sister to gather the windfalls for cider," Ma said. "She can do that while staring at worms."

I coughed again, harder this time. Ma and Hezzy both froze. I frowned at them.

"Are you ill?" Ma's voice rose sharply.

I shook my head. I felt another cough coming on but shut my lips against it. My nose itched. I sneezed.

Ma got up from the loom. "Your eyes are swollen," she said. "You should have spoke."

"Truly I feel well."

"There's a wind from the west." Hezzy shut the door. She reached above the loom and swung the paper window closed. The cabin darkened.

"No, don't!" I said. "The wind doesn't make me ill."

"Something does," Hezzy said.

Ma studied me. "Some say mullein leaves cure congestion," she said, "or onion poultices to the chest."

"Onions didn't help her last year," Hezzy said. "What does Ma Silver say?"

Ma Silver was a midwife, newly come to our area. She grew herbs and doctored some when she wasn't busy birthing. Our old midwife had died—good riddance, some said. She had smelled of rum, and her cures rarely healed anyone. Ma Silver had birthed Mrs. Farah's last baby, and Mrs. Farah spoke well of her.

Our ma shook her head. "I will ask," she said.

I minded the Gospel message that we should be full of hope in the Lord. I said, "Perhaps this year won't be so bad." I didn't believe my own words. Dread filled me, fear of what lay ahead.

Ma put her hand to my forehead. "Perhaps we will go to Jonesborough. There is a doctor there."

I hated Jonesborough. I hated the noise and stink of so many people. "Take Hezzy," I said. "She wishes to see the fine folk. I would rather stay here."

Hezzy snorted and went out. Hezzy would soon be thirteen. Of all of us she was the only one to care for finery, the only one to dream of silk dresses and sweetmeats. Hezzy was often impatient with me.

Ma smiled gently. For a moment she pressed my head against her bosom. "Poor Lizzy," she said. "My poor daughter."

I laid my knife on the table and put my arms around Ma. Her hard round belly poked my side. We had a baby coming, near Christmas we hoped. "What can't be cured must be endured," I whispered. 'Twas what Ma often said.

"'Tis true," Ma answered, "yet we will cure you if we may."

She went back to the loom. "Don't work more than you feel able," she said. "If you take a spell, rest for a while."

"I won't take a spell," I said. I cut an apple in half with one stroke and smothered another cough on the back of my hand. Paring apples, how hard was that? While Nan and Hezzy worked outside in the sun.

Chapter Two

That night Pa came in beaming. "Look," he said, holding up a fine string of fish. Trout, good smoked but better fresh. Nan raked coals onto the hearth and set the skillet to heat while Hezzy and Ma gutted the fish. I sat small in the corner. Not even fish could cheer me.

Pa sat on the chair and took off his boots. He waggled his toes by the fire. He rumpled my hair. "What's amiss, puss?" he said. "And why do we have the windows closed on this hot night?"

"My fault," I whispered.

"She's taken ill again," Ma said sharply.

"'Tis not your fault." Nan knelt beside me.

"No," Pa said after a moment. "Not your fault, Lizzy. Well, we'll be keeping the windows closed then."

"I thought of the Jonesborough doctor," said Ma. She laid a fish in the hot fat in the pan. It sizzled and spattered.

"Aye," Pa said. "Can you finish the coverlet quickly?"

"Aye," Ma said.

I did not understand what they meant then, but in the night as I lay awake between Hezzy and Nan it came to me. The price of the coverlet would pay the doctor.

That coverlet was two months' work for all of us. Pa had sheared the sheep and grown the flax. Ma, Hezzy, Nan, and I had made the flax into linen thread for the warp—a long and tiresome process—and carded and spun the fleece into wool thread for the weft. We had so looked forward to the pig that the coverlet would buy.

Hezzy snored softly. Moonlight filtered through the cracks between the shingles. The bed ropes creaked as Ma rolled over. "Lizzy, go to sleep," she murmured. "Save your worries for the morning."

IN THE MORNING I could not open my eyes. The phlegm that oozed out from between my eyelids had dried and matted my lashes together. I spat on my fingers and rubbed until the lashes came free. I sat up. I was alone in the cabin. The fire had been stirred and the water buckets filled. I went to the door and looked out. Pa was leading the horses to the stream. Nan was scattering corn for the chickens. I ran out to her. "Why did no one wake me?"

She shrugged. "Ma said," she answered.

"I am not an invalid," I said. "I won't be."

Nan frowned. "You look awful," she said. "You've got snot all down your shift. What happened to your eyes?"

" 'Tis just the same as last year," I said. "Don't you remember?"

Nan shut her mouth into a line. I could see that she remembered. "I'd stay in the house," she said. "You might start breakfast."

I went back to the house. I put on my petticoat, rinsed my face, and made corn bread and tea. When Ma came in she pulled the coverlet off her own bed, shook the dust from it, and wrapped it in a large piece of brown paper. "We don't need this in hot weather," she said. I was not surprised when she added, "We're going to Jonesborough today."

CHAPTER THREE

Jonesborough was as crowded and ugly as always. Horses and wagons clogged the streets, filling the air with silty brown dust. Men shouted. A stagecoach rattled by, three men clinging to its top. Hezzy tried so hard to see who or what was inside it that she nearly went over the side of our wagon. We had all gone together in the end. Hezzy yearned so for excitement, and Nan would not be left behind.

The storekeeper took Ma's coverlet and paid her in cash, ten bits, not as much as we had hoped. " 'Twould be more in trade," he offered cheerfully. He had pigs in the yard behind the store. I could smell them. I hated my cough, my eyes.

Hezzy fingered the row of silk ribbons on the counter. Nan looked all about, eyes full of wonder. I choked just then and brought up a huge knot of phlegm. Pa passed me his handkerchief so I could spit it out. I wiped my eyes. They itched worse the more I rubbed them. The storekeeper looked sympathetic and handed Ma the coins without another word.

The doctor had an office on the main street. He had a room just for sitting in, full of wood-backed chairs, with whitewashed walls and a real glass window looking onto the street. Hezzy stood and watched. "'Tis the woman from the stagecoach!" she cried. "Look, Nan! What a gown she's wearing. Oh!"

Nan looked. "There's a lad with her," she observed.

Hezzy's face turned pink. I guessed the lad might be handsome. Hezzy had started to think of such things.

"Daughter, sit down," Pa commanded. Ma put her arm around my shoulder and let me lean into her. Hezzy sat, looking ashamed.

The inner door opened and the doctor came in. He was not large, but he was so fine and elegant that he seemed to fill the room. He wore lace ruffles at his wrists and neck. He had silver buttons on his waistcoat. He looked too grand to talk to, until he smiled and his smile also filled the room. "This must be my patient," he said, bowing low over my hand.

"Sir," I whispered. "How do you do?"

"Better, I believe, than you, child," he said. "But we will fix that."

The doctor led us all into his examining room. He looked into my nose and eyes. He leaned his head against my chest and listened to my heartbeat. He felt my pulse. "She has no fever," he said. "She does not seem to suffer from an excess of blood." My parents nodded. "But as you see, she suffers from a great excess of phlegm; her head and chest are full of it." Again my parents nodded. I nodded too. I felt full of phlegm.

"The old midwife said 'twas asthma," Hezzy said. "She made Lizzy an onion poultice."

Ma shook her head at Hezzy for speaking out of turn, but the doctor looked at her kindly. "Yes, asthma," he said. "You can hear it in her lungs. But you can see she does not suffer from asthma alone. Her eyes and nose are affected too." He smiled grandly. "The cause, dear child, is an excess of phlegm." He turned to Ma and Pa. "The thing we must do is purge her."

The doctor shook some brown powder into a small glass. He added water from a pitcher, stirred with his finger, and handed it to me. I drank it down. Then the doctor held a basin for me while I vomited again and again, until my sides ached and my stomach writhed.

"There you are," the doctor said gently. He wiped

my face with a cloth and gave me some water to rinse my mouth. I dared not swallow it. "Keep her quiet at home," he told my parents, "and bring her back whenever she may need it. Do you live in town?"

They explained that we had a two-hour journey. He nodded and wrapped a packet of purging powders for my mother to take with us. Lastly he named his fee—one Spanish dollar. My mouth fell open. Almost all the coverlet money gone.

When we were out on the street Hezzy said bitterly, "A whole dollar! We could have puked her at home for free."

The stagecoach was standing near where we had hitched our wagon. As Pa lifted me into the wagon, and handed up Hezzy and Nan, a lady stepped out of one of the buildings and came toward the coach. Her wide gown was as blue as the sky in winter, and ribbons trailed from her sleeves. Beside her walked a tall, golden-haired lad, elegantly clad, his hand at her elbow. He looked of an age to be her son.

"Look, Hezzy!" Nan cried loudly. "'Tis the lady we saw from the window!"

Hezzy blushed and looked away. The lady looked at us and smiled, a gentle smile. The lad grinned. He helped the woman into the coach and climbed in after her. The driver cracked his whip. The horses started, and the coach rattled off ahead of us.

Pa leaned back in the wagon seat. "May as well let them get ahead," he said. "We don't want to be eating their dust all the way home." We lived not far off the stagecoach road.

I lay down on the straw in the wagon bed. I felt dizzy and weak, and worse than ever.

"He was a pretty boy," Nan said to Hezzy mischievously. "Prettier than Charlie, think you not?"

"Hush," Hezzy said. She blushed deeper. Charlie Smithson was the son of one of our nearest neighbors. He was fourteen, thick-limbed and clumsy. Hezzy thought he smelled like an ox. He seemed to fancy her anyhow. Some days he came to our farm and sat for ages, not speaking, just watching her.

"Think you, Hezzy?" Nan persisted.

" 'Twill not matter," Hezzy said in a strange, soft voice. "He's gone."

Pa looked back at us for a long moment. Then he did an odd thing. He handed the reins to Ma, climbed from the wagon and marched into the store where we'd sold the coverlet. He came back with a small parcel wrapped in brown paper and handed it to Hezzy. I thought it would be a silk ribbon, but it was a small wooden fife. Hezzy blew into it and it peeped. She fiddled with it all the long ride home, and by the time we got there she could play something very much like a song.

CHAPTER FOUR

That night a thunderstorm raged over our farm. We pulled all the shutters tight, but water still sputtered around the edges of the windows. The fire smoked and hissed. Thunder boomed. I huddled by the fire, shivering. I hated storms.

Ma put her hand to my forehead. "Feeling better?" she asked.

'Twas my duty to feel better, after the expense and trouble of the doctor. I bowed my head. "Not yet," I replied.

Ma nodded. "Perhaps in the morning," she said. "To bed, now."

I wiped my nose and coughed. "I can't sleep," I said. "Not when it's raining so hard."

"I can't sleep either," Nan complained. "Lizzy coughs too much."

"Stay awake, then," Pa grunted. "No hurry." He sat in the chair and lit his pipe. Tobacco smoke mingled with the smoke from the fire.

"I can sleep." Hezzy pulled our underbed out from our parents' bed and burrowed under the covers. Ma got into bed as well and lay on her side with her arms over her belly.

I sat on the stool in front of our spinning wheel. I started the treadle and began to spin. We had a sheep whose wool was finer than all the rest, and Nan and I had picked out the finest parts of her fleece. When Ma finished the coverlet on the loom, she would weave a new blanket with the best wool for the baby.

Nan pulled a bench to my side. "I'll card for you," she said. So she sat and carded the soft wool into rolags, and I spun the rolags into yarn. With my hands to the wheel I could not wipe my nose, but every now and again Nan would put her quick hand out and pat my face with Ma's kerchief. Pa smoked. Ma and Hezzy lay and watched the fire. I could see their eyes shining, and I knew they did not sleep.

I stopped to cough. Nan stopped carding and waited for me. "Are you better yet, Lizzy?" Hezzy whispered.

"Quiet," Pa said softly, as though to the fire.

Suddenly someone pounded on the door. I jumped. The wool in my hands sucked itself onto the bobbin. Nan flew up, knocking over the bench, and Pa took his musket from its pegs before opening the door. Nan and I, Hezzy and Ma too peeked around Pa to see who it could be.

A man stood on the step, water streaming from his hat and greatcoat. "Your servant, sir," he said. "I humbly beg your pardon for intruding on your family in the night."

Pa was not used to folk who spoke like gentry. He swung the door open wider but kept his musket ready. Light from the fire shone on our visitor's face. He was a Negro, his face as dark as the stormy night.

The man held up a tin box he was carrying. "My mistress sent me to ask you, might we beg a bit of fire? Our tinderbox has been wet through, and she craves something warm to drink."

Pa stood still for a moment. He studied the man's calm face. Ma climbed over the edge of the underbed and reached for her shawl. Pa made up his mind. He opened the door wide. "Come in."

The man stepped inside and pulled off his hat. "Step by the fire," Hezzy said, "you're dripping into our bed." She moved up to the edge of the big bed and pulled Ma's blanket over the shoulders of her shift. The man apologized softly and moved to the hearth.

Ma pulled the kettle over the flames and asked the man to have a drink.

He shook his head. "I'll be hurrying back, if it please you, ma'am. The mistress does be expecting me."

"And who, sir, is your mistress?" Pa's voice was gravelly. I saw that he did not yet trust this stranger.

"Mistress Beaumont, sir," he said. "Wife to Mr. Beaumont, both arrived this day. They have business in the territory, sir, with the governor, so they say. There is a cabin just east of here where they intend to stay for some time."

The new governor lived far east of here, east of Jonesborough, even, in what folks called the finest house in the territory. The only cabin I knew of just east of our farm was a ramshackle log pile long abandoned by early settlers. I could imagine how uncomfortable it might be on a wet dark night. "Spiders," I said, then was surprised to realize I'd spoken aloud.

The man smiled at me. "Yes, miss, the logs are crawling," he said. "We are anxious for a fire."

Pa shoveled coals into the man's box. "And your name, sir?" he asked.

The man took the box. "Daniel, sir," he said. He put on his hat and opened the door.

Pa put his hand against the door frame. "Daniel?"

"Just, Daniel, sir," the man said, and was gone.

CHAPTER FIVE

In the morning my eyes were not glued shut. I opened them freely, sat up, and looked around. The cabin was shrouded in soft gray shadows, and rain thrummed steadily against the roof. Nan opened her eyes and looked at me. I smiled.

"You're better!" Nan sat up and grinned. She shook Hezzy's shoulder. "Lizzy's better!"

Hezzy's eyes flew open. "Aye, she looks better," she said. "The puking worked, then."

My chest no longer felt painfully tight. My eyes still itched, but not so badly. I found I could breathe through my nose. "The puking worked," I said, and laughed out loud.

All that morning it rained, and we were happy. Pa did chores and worked in the barn. Ma wove and wove, the loom creaking and thumping. Nan carded, I spun. Hezzy moved restlessly about the cabin. She stirred the fire. She cooked a pie. She nibbled her fingernails. Finally she sat at the table with a bit of pencil and the paper her flute had been wrapped in. "What are you doing?" Nan asked.

"Nothing so far," she said.

A bit later, however, she showed the paper to Ma. Ma frowned at it, then nodded. " 'Twould be pretty," she said.

"Can we?" Hezzy asked.

"Perhaps," Ma said. "We'll see."

Hezzy sighed in frustration. She smoothed her paper under her hand. "We should try. We should do different things."

"What is it?" Nan asked again.

"Nothing," Hezzy said.

Ma cleared her throat. She spoke above the sound of the loom. "Your sister has drawn a new coverlet pattern," she said. "We will try it someday."

Nan and I stopped our work to look at it. The marks did not make sense to me: I was not yet good at weaving, and I could only see patterns once they were started in the cloth. Nan smiled as though she understood. Perhaps she did. "Very nice," she said.

Still Hezzy looked dissatisfied. I wished she had

never caught a glimpse of the fine lady in Jonesborough. Hezzy had trouble enough being satisfied.

I spun out another rolag into fine creamy thread. The grease from the wool softened my hands. I loved to spin. 'Twas a lucky thing, since I did so much of it.

"We should bleach some of our linen this year too," Hezzy said suddenly. Nan giggled.

"'Tis such a lot of work," Ma said, shaking her head.

I had never bleached linen before, but I knew it took months, and piles of cow manure. Of that we had plenty.

"I'll do it all," Hezzy said. "By myself."

"We'll see," Ma said.

Hezzy made an exasperated sound between her teeth. She snatched her flute from the table and ran out into the rain. I pushed the window open a crack to see where she went. She was standing at the top of the ridge, staring east as though she could see Jonesborough through the clouds.

Nan put down the carders. She picked up her doll, Florence, who had been sitting in the basket of wool. She cuddled Florence. "When the baby comes, we'll feed it and rock it and sing it to sleep," she said.

"Aye," said Ma.

Outside, Hezzy stood, waiting. Suddenly the heavy clouds moved apart and a single ray of sunshine shot to the ground. Hezzy raised her hands. She put the flute to her lips and, piping, began to dance.

CHAPTER SIX

"Who do you think Mistress Beaumont is?" Hezzy asked the next day. The rain continued. My chest was clear. Ma had finished the coverlet pieces and was ready to take them off the loom. Mrs. Smithson, Charlie's mother, had come to call and was helping Ma.

"Another midwife," Nan said with a giggle.

Hezzy looked at her scornfully. "Who has business with the governor!" she said.

"Sweep the floor, Nan," Ma cut in. "You've tracked in dirt." To Mrs. Smithson she added, "I told you about Daniel, but I can't think who these Beaumonts could be. Fine folk wouldn't likely stay in that cabin. Common folk wouldn't likely see the governor."

"Speculators," Mrs. Smithson said. She meant folks who bought and sold land. The Southwest Territory was full of them.

Hezzy frowned. "He spoke well for a servant."

"It can't matter to us," I said.

"No," said Ma.

Hezzy was spinning, but she let the wheel stop. "Do you suppose he's a slave or indentured?"

"Indentured," Nan guessed. Indentured servants were bound to their masters for seven years, to pay their passage to America, or learn a trade, or pay some other debt. They were like slaves, except that their servitude had an end. White folks were more likely to be indentured and Negroes more likely to be slaves, but I had seen indentured Negroes, and free ones too. There were some in Jonesborough. Pa had pointed one out to me, years back.

"It can't matter," I repeated. "If the Beaumonts have servants, they're too fine for us."

Hezzy pursed her lips. "Perhaps they go to the Methodist church."

Mrs. Smithson laughed. "If they do, we'll see them sure on Sunday." We were all Methodists near-by. The church was close enough to walk to, and Pa said the preaching was as good there as at any other.

THE BEAUMONTS did go to the Methodist church. I saw Daniel out the window after we were already sitting in our pew. He was standing beneath a tree with some other men. The rain had stopped at last, and a stiff wind blew from the west. My shoes were wet from the grass. They felt cold and stiff on my feet. The church smelled of damp.

My eyes were itching again. I didn't like to think of that.

I elbowed Hezzy, who sat beside me. Instead of looking out the window where I pointed, she darted a glance over her shoulder. Hezzy gasped. I stole a look over my shoulder too. A woman I did not know stood in the doorway in an elegant gown. She looked round for a seat, and so did the tall boy beside her. I recognized the boy just as Hezzy jerked her head back. Her cheeks flamed.

"The lady from the coach?" I whispered.

Hezzy nodded. "I think she must be Daniel's mistress. That Mrs. Beaumont."

The service seemed longer than usual. Hezzy squirmed and fidgeted, though she dared not look behind her. I held perfectly still. I could feel my illness creeping back. I tried not to move at all, as if being still would cure me.

Hezzy and I were both disappointed. After the service Daniel's mistress left before anyone could do more than admire the color of her gown, and by nightfall I was sicker than I had been before our trip to Jonesborough.

CHAPTER SEVEN

For several days, Ma used the powder from the doctor to puke me morning and night. I grew faintheaded. When I lay down my nose and mouth filled so that I could not breathe. Pa cushioned our chair with bags of straw and I slept there, upright, my feet on the bench in front of me. My eyes burned and ran. Worst of all, my chest tightened. My sides ached. I fought to breathe.

On the third day Ma looked at Pa. "Ma Silver," she said. Pa nodded and went out the door.

"She won't help," Hezzy said. "'Twill be like last year. Those onion poultices did no good."

"Hezzy," warned Ma. She bathed my eyes with a wet rag.

"We should make that doctor come here," Hezzy

said. "Midwives don't know anything. Just about babies, that's all."

"Hezzy, hush," Ma said.

"I hear she's part Cherokee," Hezzy said.

"Be quiet!" 'Twas the first I'd spoken all day. I coughed and wiped my nose on my shift. "I'll not go back to that doctor. I will not!" I didn't know what had gotten into Hezzy.

Hezzy wrapped her arms around me. "I'm sorry, sister," she said. " 'Tis only that I'm worried for you. I'm sorry."

"I don't want to be puked anymore," I said.

Nan spoke from the corner, where she was wiping the breakfast dishes. "Lay down, Ma. We'll watch her close until Ma Silver comes."

Whenever I had woken from coughing, Ma had had her arms around me. Mrs. Hough and Mrs. Smithson had both been by to cook for us. They made broth we kept on the fire. But 'twas Ma who fed me sips all night through. I did not want her to sleep now. "I want Ma," I said.

"Shhh," Hezzy said, her arms still around me. "She needs to rest. She's that tired. Think of the baby."

I struggled against Hezzy. I wanted my mother. Hezzy held me tight. "I will be with you," she said. She took my hand, and I gripped it hard.

The house seemed too quiet. 'Twas dark like wintertime, because Hezzy insisted we keep the paper windows shut. "Ma said so," she said. Ma slept motionless on the bed. Nan made corncakes and stewed vegetables for dinner. Hezzy sat beside me. She wiped my face and held my hand. I had never known her to sit still for so long.

After dinner Suzy Pearlette and her mother came to call. Suzy furrowed her brow when she saw me. "Mrs. Smithson said you was bad off," she said. "You look bad off."

"Help with the dishes, and hush with your mouth," Mrs. Pearlette said. "See ye that Mrs. Baker is sleeping?" Suzy stacked the dinner dishes in the washtub. She looked at me and bit her lip. I closed my eyes.

"Ma needs to sleep," Hezzy whispered.

"Aye," Mrs. Pearlette said. "And so you should have fetched me, Hezzy, before you let her get so tired."

Hezzy did not tell her that it was my fault, that I had wanted Ma. "Pa went to get Ma Silver," she said.

Mrs. Pearlette nodded. "She helped Mrs. Hough's Edward when he had that fever," she said. "Don't fret, Hezzy. She's some better at healing than old Nancy was."

"I found a fairy ring in the woods, Lizzy," Suzy

said. "When you're better we'll go see if 'tis still there."

"Aye," I whispered without opening my eyes.

"WHAT'S AMISS, DEARIE?" Ma Silver bellowed as she came through the door. She was so large a person— tall, broad-shouldered, and wide—that the cabin seemed to shrink around her. Even Pa was small by her side. She moved big too. She threw a sack on the table and knelt in front of me. Her petticoats swished against the floor. Hezzy and Mrs. Pearlette got out of the way. Ma Silver put her hands on each side of my face and pulled my eyes open with her broad flat thumbs. Her hands felt cool and strong. "Dearie, dearie," she said, shaking her head. "Let's see what we can do."

Ma Silver moved fast despite her size. She opened her sack and brought out bundles of herbs. She sent my sisters and Suzy scurrying to the garden for more. She woke Ma and spoke to her rapidly, explaining her actions as she worked. She snapped at Pa and Mrs. Pearlette to bring water and wood.

Within minutes, it seemed, I was drinking a steaming cup of unfamiliar sharp-tasting tea. A cloth filled with chopped cucumber was tied round my eyes, and another cloth held a burning poultice to my back. Ma

Silver smeared goose fat across my chapped nose and lips. She pulled off the poultice and bent me over her knee. *Thump! Thump! Thump!* She clapped her huge hands hard against my back. I coughed and brought up phlegm.

"That's it, dearie," Ma Silver said. "Do that again."

She pounded and I coughed. For a few minutes I felt better. Then I began to struggle for breath under the weight of her hands. Ma Silver noticed. She pulled me up and settled me back in the chair. "Hurts, does it?"

I pressed my hand against my ribs. "All here, when I breathe," I said. "'Tis work to breathe."

"Aye, I've seen it before," she said. "Your lungs sound like a tin whistle."

Pa looked at Ma and Hezzy. "Asthma, is it?" he asked.

Ma Silver looked up. "Aye, right enough," she said. "That sound in the lungs. The rest is something else again."

Hezzy said, "The Jonesborough doctor said she had too much phlegm."

Ma Silver spread more goose fat across my face. "Aye, mebbe so," she said. "Mebbe not. Why should one person get sick and another stay healthy? Nobody knows. You see what I do here, Mrs. Baker? I'll bring by some of my salve, keep her lips from getting so chapped." Ma Silver gently tied the strings on my shift. "The lungs is the worst," she said. "Her nose, eyes, they discomfort her, but 'tis the lungs you must watch for. She's got to be able to breathe." She patted my shoulder. "Don't fret, dearie. I've seen this pass."

"Me too," I whispered. I pushed the cucumber rag up a bit.

"Happened before, has it?"

"Every fall." I pulled the rag back down and, for a few hours, drifted into sleep.

CHAPTER EIGHT

If I had not known already how grievous sick I was, I could have guessed it by the number of people who came to our house. By nightfall Mrs. Hough and Mrs. Farah were sharing our fire. They took turns sitting close to me, and if I started to struggle in my sleep they woke me and pounded on my back the way Ma Silver had directed before she left. They cooked and consoled Ma. They watched and waited. Sometimes they sang hymns.

In the morning Mrs. Hough left and Mrs. Cole came. Mrs. Farah took a turn sleeping, then did a wash for Ma. Charlie Smithson chopped kindling outside our door. I saw him while Ma changed the dressing on my eyes. The cucumbers eased them, and the goose fat eased my skin, but nothing anyone did eased my breathing. I was grateful no one puked me.

Early on Nan put my doll, Sarah, into my arms. I held her tight, but not because I cared for her. I had no interest in dolls now. Sarah was soft, stuffed with rags, and I could squeeze her without hurting her. When I held people's hands they pulled away.

Later Nan tucked her doll, Florence, in beside me too. When I took a coughing spasm Florence fell to the hearth. Her hair smoldered. Nan took her back without saying a word.

Ma Silver came and went as she could. Many folks called upon her, even coming to our house. She had a small spotted horse she rode about the country. Each time she came back to our cabin over the next few days she brought a new herb to try—mullein, tansy, chamomile—and under her cool hands I could sometimes relax for a moment or two. Mostly every part of me felt tight and strained. If I didn't keep working, I would not breathe. When I stopped breathing I would die.

Hezzy took to sitting on the floor beside my chair. She rested her head against my arm. "I can't do this," I whispered to her one night. Ma and Pa and Nan were in bed. Mrs. Smithson snored softly by the fire.

Hezzy didn't look up. "You must," she said.

"Hezzy." My words staggered out between painful

breaths. "I can't do it much longer. I want to. But truly I can't."

She did not respond.

THE NEXT MORNING Hezzy thrust something into my hand. My eyes were covered with another cucumber rag. I felt smooth wood, carved into a shape. "What is it?" I asked.

"A horse." Hezzy sounded scornful. "Charlie carved it. As if a toy horse could help you."

"Nice of him."

"We don't need more kindling, but he doesn't go away."

I began to cough. This time Ma pounded my back. Hezzy walked away.

WE HAD TWO days of rain and on the second I revived somewhat, though not as much as before. Afterward the air was cooler but the wind blew harder. I was as sick as ever. Still the neighbors came, every day, taking on as much of our burden as they could. I became less and less aware of them. All I thought of was breathing. I wanted desperately to sleep but I was afraid to. I knew I was going to die.

One morning I became dimly aware of another

person in the cabin, who spoke with Ma a few moments and then left. "Daniel's mistress," Hezzy whispered. "Mrs. Beaumont. The woman from the coach."

"And . . . was she . . . nicely . . . dressed?"

"I didn't notice," Hezzy said.

NAN MUST HAVE been there, helping, all the time. Ma, I know, never left my side. The other women took their turns. But the last day I was only truly aware of Hezzy.

I knew I could not fight much longer. I felt my strength failing. I could not even cough. Each breath meant only that I would have to breathe again. I did not want to do it anymore.

But there was Hezzy beside me, Hezzy holding my hand. Hezzy was so strong she seemed to give me strength; enough, at least, to breathe, and breathe again. The cabin grew colder. Someone poked at the fire, and it blazed up, lighting the cabin walls. Hezzy moved herself into the chair with me. She cradled my head against her chest and rubbed her hand over my back again and again.

"You mustn't sleep," she said, her voice soft and loving. "Mustn't sleep, Lizzy, Lizzy dear."

Night grew deeper and deeper. Cold air seeped in

through the walls. I felt as if we were completely alone. We were locked in a battle against death, Hezzy and me, and even though I knew for certain that death would win, I was grateful for Hezzy's company. Night passed. "Mustn't sleep, Lizzy dear."

At last I could not stay awake. I slept, cradled against Hezzy. I drifted into darkness. And then I heard a loud bang, like the crash of a pot lid. I opened my eyes. Pa stood by the fire looking sheepish. He had dropped a pot lid on the hearth. Mrs. Hough was looking at him too, and smiling. 'Twas morning. The sky was bright and the air bitterly cold. My sides were still weary but my breath came easier. My nose and eyes felt clear. 'Twas over. I might live. "Pa!" I said, and he came toward me, smiling. Beneath me, Hezzy slept on.

CHAPTER NINE

Frost had killed the garden in the night. The plants lay in blackened, melting heaps. After kissing me and exclaiming over me, patting me and even crying a little, Ma took Nan and went out before breakfast to pick what vegetables might be saved.

Pa carried me to the bed and laid me down. I sank into the soft straw tick. 'Twas a blessed feeling to lie flat after sitting in the chair for so long. Mrs. Hough kissed me gently before she left. "Lord bless and keep you, child," she said.

Pa laid Hezzy beside me. "Do ye need anything, Lizzy?" he asked.

I shook my head. "No, Pa."

"Well, then. We'll be back shortly, eh?" He took a basket and went out to help Ma. I felt bone-weary, but much too happy to sleep. The slant of light through the greased-paper windows, the smell of smoke from the fire, the skeins of soft wool hung on the walls, all seemed wonderful to me.

Nan came in rubbing her eyes, her cap and kerchief askew. "Hezzy should be helping," she said.

"Hezzy should be sleeping," I replied. "She stayed up the night through. She kept me alive."

Nan made a sour face. "Pa said maybe 'twas the weather that saved you. He said 'twas the earliest frost he'd ever seen."

"Maybe." I didn't know. Could harvesttime cause my wheezing? Did my sickness just happen to end on a cold, cold night? "Let Hezzy sleep anyway," I said.

Nan plopped herself down on the edge of the bed frame. The ropes sagged. "I would have stayed awake for you too," she said.

"I know that," I replied.

IN MY ILLNESS I left my childhood behind. I did not realize it right away. But in the days that followed, as I lay or sat about the cabin, still recovering, I saw that I had lost my taste for childish play. When Nan brought our dolls to the bed and playacted some fantastical game, I could not join her with the same spirit. The dolls were just dolls, stuffed rags really; I cared more for Nan and her sharp bright face, more for the unborn babe kicking in Ma's belly. Nan and I had always played together, but I felt closer to Hezzy now. Sometimes Nan looked puzzled and sad.

We talked about what had caused my illness but came no closer to understanding it. Ma Silver listened at my chest and said I was surely better but could not say why. "God's will," she offered.

"The frost?" Pa asked.

"Mebbe," Ma Silver said. "Why do you think so?"

"She's usually better once cold weather comes," Ma said.

"I wasn't sick in Pennsylvania," I said.

"Aye, you were," Ma said, smoothing back my hair. "Not so bad, but you were. Every fall."

"All's well that ends well," Ma Silver said, smiling, as she went out the door.

'TWAS NOT LONG before I grew strong enough to walk about the farm. The air was still crisp and cold; the sky was bright blue and the tree-covered mountains were red and orange. Hezzy walked with me.

"The fine lady came while you were sick," she said.

"Aye, I remember," I said. "You didn't notice her dress."

"She wanted something, she didn't say what. She didn't know you were sick until she came."

"Who would tell her?" I asked.

Hezzy shrugged. "Everyone else knew," she said.

WHEN THE FINE LADY, Mrs. Beaumont, returned a few days later, I understood why she had not heard the news. I was spinning and Ma was at the loom. Nan and Hezzy were outside, turning the piles of flax on the grass. The lady paused in the open doorway and tapped her hand lightly against the wood. She did not walk in as a neighbor would.

I stopped the wheel and Ma stopped the loom. Ma bobbed her head at the lady. I did nothing.

"Good morning," Mrs. Beaumont said, her voice soft like water.

"Good morning, madam," Ma said, stiff and polite. Ma never used such a tone with her friends.

Mrs. Beaumont hesitated in the doorway. "May I come in?"

"Of certain, ma'am." Ma got up and adjusted the chair in front of the hearth. She sat down on a bench.

Mrs. Beaumont came in. She walked with a graceful, ladylike, elegant air, and when she sat her back did not touch the back of the chair. She wore a full gown with a pattern woven into the cloth, one I had seen before at church. 'Twas the color of wine, and I longed to touch it to see if it felt as soft as it looked. Her petticoat was gray. Lace trailed from her elegant cap. I thought she could walk into any grand house anywhere with perfect ease, yet she did not look easy in our cabin. I understood why Ma did not make her more welcome.

"My name is Sarah Beaumont," she said, holding out her hand.

Ma shook it. "Hannah Baker, madam," she said. Again she bobbed her head. I began to grow angry at Mrs. Beaumont for making Ma act so. "Would you like some tea?"

"Thank you," Mrs. Beaumont answered. "I should like some indeed."

I stood. "I'll fetch Hezzy," I said. Hezzy would not want to miss this. Ma nodded.

Hezzy and Nan came in, their aprons and hands stained from the rotting stalks of flax. Hezzy's cheeks flamed up when she saw Mrs. Beaumont. She unpinned her apron quickly and doused her hands in the bucket by the door. Nan merely stared. She slid to the floor, still staring.

Mother introduced us round, and the fine lady smiled. "How do you do, Mrs. Beaumont?" Hezzy said. She dropped a graceful curtsey. Mrs. Beaumont's smile widened.

"You must call me Miss Sarah," she said. "We are from Charleston, you know. 'Tis custom there."

Hezzy took over the tea making. Ma sat stiff and upright like our visitor. Nan and I looked at each other. Several times Miss Sarah seemed about to speak, but she did not. The silence grew more and more uncomfortable.

Finally I thought of something to say. I asked, "Is Daniel indentured or a slave?"

"Lizzy!" Hezzy hissed.

Miss Sarah—if we were truly to call her that, which I found hard to believe—did not seem discomforted. "He is a slave belonging to my husband," she said, easily enough. "We have a small plantation north of Charleston. We grow indigo there, and some rice. Daniel and Cook accompanied us on this journey."

'Twas a long answer to a simple question, but it enabled us to start talking. Ma asked why the Beaumonts had come to the territory. Miss Sarah explained that they were here for a few months only, until spring perhaps, while Mr. Beaumont surveyed and purchased land. He was a speculator, then, as we had guessed.

Pa often said you couldn't throw a stick in the Southwest Territory without you'd hit a speculator on the head. He said now that the Indian treaties were in place and all the Cherokee had left for other parts, and we were organized into a territory and all, folks would come here from everywhere wanting a piece of land to farm. Land speculators were those who bought huge pieces of land from the government, carved them into farms, and sold them one by one.

"Mr. Beaumont's son, William, my stepson, travels with us," Miss Sarah said.

Ma asked if Miss Sarah had children of her own. Miss Sarah said that she did not. Ma commented that the cabin Miss Sarah was living in was sure to be drafty come winter. Miss Sarah said brightly that it was turning out fine. Daniel had fixed it up for them. "I do so love an adventure," she said. "'Tis such a treat to be away from Charleston for a while. Society can be so confining."

Hezzy's eyes widened. She poured Miss Sarah and Ma another cup of tea. Then she sat down as close to Miss Sarah as she could and stared at her dress. On the floor, Nan slurped her tea. Hezzy glared at her.

"I don't believe we've seen Mr. Beaumont at church," Ma said politely.

Miss Sarah flushed. "He is a dedicated churchgoer," she said. "He has been gone to Fort Knox since a few days after settling us in the cabin." There was a small silence. "William stays with me," Miss Sarah said. "And Daniel is always on guard."

Again a silence grew. Ma sat. Finally Miss Sarah said, "I hear from the shopkeepers in Jonesborough that you weave coverlets for sale."

"Aye," said Ma.

"I hoped that I might trouble you to weave one for me."

"Aye," Ma said. "I would be glad to." They talked for a few minutes about the particulars of the coverlet, about Miss Sarah not having her own wool for trade, about the bright colors she wanted to make her cabin cheerful. Miss Sarah slipped her hand into her fancy pocket and brought out some coins.

"To begin with," she said. "To purchase the wool."

"Thank you, madam." Ma did not mention that we would be using our own wool, the wool I was spinning most like.

Miss Sarah took another sip of tea and set her mug down firmly. "Good day to you all," she said. She gathered her skirts around her, stood, and left.

"Why didn't you ask her to stay to dinner?" Hezzy asked Ma.

"'Twas not a social call," Ma said. "'Twas business only." She went back to her loom, to the baby blanket she was weaving. "Spin well, Lizzy," she told me. "'Twill take fine work to please her."

CHAPTER TEN

I went to church again the next day. We were greeted in the churchyard with smiles and flutterings of delight from the Smithsons, the Houghs, and the rest of our neighbors who had helped to nurse me. The women crowded around me, patting my head and talking in quick words of their joy at seeing me well. Suzy Pearlette kissed my cheek. Everyone had known I was better. They had most of them been to call. But I supposed they had not expected to see me out again so soon.

As we stood near the church door a single horse came down the road. Miss Sarah rode it aside. Daniel led it, and Miss Sarah's stepson, Mr. William, walked beside him.

Miss Sarah wore a different gown, a white, floating, square-necked one sashed in blue. Mr. William had bright brass buttons down the front of his coat and silver buckles on his shoes. Daniel looked like us, his suit plain but neat and clean.

Miss Sarah alighted from the horse and Daniel led it to the shed. Ma looked toward her, then away. She said something to Mrs. Cole. Mrs. Cole answered gaily and turned her shoulders a bit to make it seem that she had not noticed Miss Sarah. All of them pretended not to notice Miss Sarah, who stood in the clearing with Mr. William by her side.

'Twas one thing not to speak to her when she came to church late and hurried away after. 'Twas another to ignore her in plain view, and after she had been to our house, too. "Do you expect to be finishing your harvest soon?" Mrs. Pearlette asked Ma.

"Ma," I whispered, "there's Miss Sarah."

"Aye, next week, if this fine weather holds," Ma answered Mrs. Pearlette.

"Don't look at her," Suzy Pearlette whispered to me.

"Ma," I said, tugging on her sleeve.

"Leave be, Lizzy," she told me.

"Hezzy?" I said. Hezzy looked at the ground.

I picked up my skirts and walked across the churchyard. "Good morning, Miss Sarah," I said loudly. "'Tis a pleasure to meet with you again." I curtseyed, as smoothly as I could.

Miss Sarah smiled. "Good morning, Lizzy," she said. "I am glad to see you again."

"Thank you," I said. I was pleased she remembered my name.

"Allow me to introduce my stepson, William Beaumont," Miss Sarah said.

Mr. William bowed from the waist. He was as slim and elegant as a young birch tree. "Your servant, miss," he said. He smiled politely, with perfect manners, but his eyes danced in a most impolite and appealing way.

Hezzy and Nan ran up to us. Miss Sarah remembered their names as well and introduced them to Mr. William, who bowed again. He took hold of Hezzy's hand as he did so. She giggled, then blushed scarlet. Mr. William took no notice. He tucked Hezzy's hand under his arm and escorted her into the church. He did it very properly, taking her to our pew, then walking back to sit with Miss Sarah in the rear, but still it seemed a bold gesture. Every eye in the congregation rested on Hezzy for that moment. Hezzy sang the opening hymn as happily as a bird.

ON THE WAY home Pa scolded us. "We ought to act neighborly," he said, "but you girls had no right to make a spectacle of yourselves. 'Twas shameful."

I could not tell by that speech whether Pa thought Ma should have been more welcoming, but clearly he thought I should have been less so.

"They are our closest neighbors now," I said.

"Aye." Pa shook his head at me. "But don't expect much from them. It's not living close that makes folks your neighbors."

I shut my lips. Miss Sarah had looked so lonely. But Hezzy leaned against me and whispered, "She remembered both our names." Ma glanced over her shoulder at Hezzy, and I saw where some trouble might lie.

CHAPTER ELEVEN

The next day, a letter was delivered to our house.

We were all in the field when it came, digging carrots and turnips out of the ground, so we did not see who brought it. Toward noontime, Ma asked Hezzy and me to go in and start dinner. Pa stood and wiped the sweat from his eyes. "All of you go in," he said. "You've stayed up with me this long."

Ma put her hands to her back as though it ached her. "Aye," she said, looking up at the blue sky.

"Rest a bit," Pa said. "The girls will get the food."

"Aye," Nan echoed, slipping her hand into Ma's. "We'll fix you a fine meal."

When we went into the cabin the letter sat square in the center of the table, weighted down with Pa's mug. Hezzy picked it up and squinted at it. She handed it to Ma. "Look," she said.

'Twas a true letter. It came with a postmark. I could not remember us getting a letter before. Ma handled it gingerly. She broke the seal and smoothed the paper out, then folded it up again.

" 'Twill have to wait," she said reluctantly. "Your pa can take it to the preacher after supper."

We none of us could read. Nor could our close neighbors, the Smithsons or the Farahs or the Houghs. Pa could sign his name, but Ma signed hers with an X.

"Miss Sarah," Hezzy said. "She might could read it. Or—Mr. William." Fine folk had time for such learning. Hezzy kept her eyes down.

"Aye," Ma said, sinking onto the bed. Her face looked gray and drawn. I felt worried too. I doubted that good news could come out of a letter. Ma handed it back to Hezzy. "Go, then. Go quickly."

Hezzy ran out the door. Without stopping to ask permission, I followed her, and so did Nan. We ran across the fields until I got a stitch in my side and started coughing, and even then we walked quickly. Soon the cabin Miss Sarah was using came to view.

'Twas much improved from the last time I had seen it. New shingles gleamed bright on the roof. The log walls had been fresh chinked, and a new split fence and roofed shed stood nearby. And oh! One of the paper windows had been replaced with glass. The extravagance of that stopped me in my tracks. "Hurry," Hezzy said, looking back at me.

Daniel was sitting on the front steps skinning a rabbit. He put down his knife and watched us come. He must have been out hunting, for a long rifle rested beside him. "Good day," he said quietly. He did not smile.

"Good day," Hezzy said, bobbing her head. "Is Miss Sarah here?"

"No, ma'am," said Daniel.

"Is young Mr. William?"

"No, ma'am. They went up to Jonesborough to see was there news from Mr. Beaumont. No one is here right now but Cook and me."

I peeked through the open door. A broad Negro woman was stirring something at the hearth. The cabin had been whitewashed, and every speck of it gleamed. The woman—Cook, I guessed—turned her back to us slowly.

Hezzy let out her breath. "When will they be back, do you know?"

Daniel shook his head. "They didn't say. A long time, maybe. They didn't tell us to keep supper." He went back to his rabbit.

Hezzy, Nan, and I looked at each other, not sure what to do. "Do we leave it here?" Nan asked. Hezzy shook her head.

Daniel set down his knife. "Is there a problem?" he asked.

"There's a letter," Nan said.

Hezzy showed it to him. "We were hoping Miss Sarah could read it. Or Mr. William. Or—Mr. Beaumont." We had not yet so much as seen him.

Daniel wiped his knife clean on the grass. He took a cloth and wiped his hands. Then he took the letter from Hezzy and opened it. " 'Dear daughter Hannah,' " he began.

We gaped at him. "You can read?" Hezzy asked.

Daniel put down the letter and gave us a long look. "Do you want to hear your letter?" he asked.

"But—" Hezzy started to speak, then clamped her mouth shut. "Please," she added.

Daniel smiled. "Mistress Beaumont, she has too much time on her hands," he said. "She teaches me every bit of nonsense she knows."

From the look on his face, I didn't think he believed reading was nonsense. I didn't believe it either.

Daniel went back to the letter. " 'Dear daughter Hannah,' " he began again.

"That's Ma," Nan whispered. I nodded. Our

mother was Hannah Baker. So the letter had come from our folks in Pennsylvania.

" 'It grieves me to send word that your mother, Martha, has died. She was stricken suddenly these two months ago, but 'twas only lately I could find the strength to have this letter writ to you—' "

Daniel stopped. Hezzy had turned white, and I felt tears rolling down my cheeks. Grandma, dear Grandma, Ma's mother. I could well remember her. I thought of the red quilt on her bed in Pennsylvania, of the sweet currant biscuits she made. Dead two months ago! And we didn't know, we were so far away.

"I'm sorry, missy," Daniel said softly. "Shall I go on?"

Hezzy nodded. "Please," she said.

THE LETTER CAME from Ma's father, our grandfather. It told us also all the news of the years since we had been gone. Ma's youngest brother was fighting Indians now, with General Wayne in the great wilderness of Indiana. Her older brother had plans to join him. Her sister, Elizabeth, whom I was named for, had been widowed, remarried, and had moved far away. No one of our family, our grandfather said, was left in Pennsylvania but him.

'Twas enough to make me dizzy, so much of such importance packed into one sheet of paper. Hezzy bade Daniel read it three times over, then recited it back to him.

"Yes, miss," he said, nodding. "You've got it."

"Thank you," she said. "We appreciate your trouble." Hezzy felt in her pocket, frowning. I wished too that we had something to give Daniel. Nan smiled. She reached into her own pocket, pulled out a handful of walnuts, and pressed them into Daniel's hand.

"Thank you, miss," Daniel said solemnly.

We walked home slowly. "What do you—" Nan began.

"Don't talk!" Hezzy said sharply. "I might forget something."

Ma was still lying down when we came in. The fire had died to embers, and a cold wind blew through the open door. Ma had her old quilt half over her and had flung her hand over her eyes. She looked at us, then closed her eyes again.

" 'Tis bad news," she said.

"Yes, Ma," said Hezzy, and told her all.

Ma cried loud and hard. She rolled onto her side, buried her face in her pillow, and sobbed. Hezzy stopped talking. She stood with her hands at her sides, eyes wide. None of us had ever seen Ma cry.

Nan knelt beside the bed. She pulled the quilt over

Ma's shoulders and tucked it around her, as Ma had done for us when we were small. "Shhh," she said, brushing Ma's cheek with her hand. Ma quit crying. She lay still with her eyes shut. She ignored us all.

Hezzy poked the fire and we made corncakes and heated a skillet for them. Nan fluttered between us and Ma. "Maybe Daniel was lying," she said softly. "Ma Silver makes up stories. Maybe Daniel does too. Maybe that wasn't really what the letter said."

Hezzy gave her a look dripping with scorn. "Ma Silver tells stories for fun," she said. "She doesn't tell lies. 'Dear daughter Hannah,' the letter said. How would Daniel have known that? How would he know all the right names? He didn't make anything up."

Nan started to cry. "I was just hoping," she said.

Hezzy tossed a corncake into the skillet. The fat spat. Hezzy jumped back. "I know," she said. "'Tis no use, is all."

I laid the dishes on the table. I filled our mugs with water. Then, with nothing else to do, I began to spin. I thought of Grandma being dead so long, and us not knowing. I thought of myself dying. I had come so close.

Suddenly I grabbed the spinning wheel and yanked it to a halt. Fear washed over me; my breath stopped and for a moment it felt as though my heart stopped too.

My sickness would come again. I had been sick at the end of every summer we had lived here, and every year I had been worse.

I could not get worse than I had been this year and still live.

At the end of next summer, I was going to die.

CHAPTER TWELVE

Ma lay in silent agony while we ate dinner. She did not sleep, or cry, or open her eyes. Even when Pa sat on the edge of the bed, chafed her hands, and said cajolingly, "Come, now, she had a good life, your mother," Ma did not respond.

"Give her time, then," Pa said quietly to us. He looked exasperated but not unkind. "You just have a rest," he said more loudly, "the girls and I will finish with those turnips."

I did not want to finish with the turnips. I was going to die! I wanted to stay and lie against Ma. I wanted to tell Pa that soon enough they would have someone else to grieve for. But I got up and went out to the field.

We worked until dark, until we were hungry and

achy, cold and tired. The cow was mooing in protest, her bag full to bursting, when Pa finally straightened his back and said we could go in. We stopped at the spring to wash our hands. I could see a light shining through the cabin windows. That was good; at least Ma had gotten out of bed to tend the fire. As we walked closer I smelled something savory and delicious.

"Stew!" Nan said, grinning in amazement. We seldom ate so much at night, but after our hard work we were powerful hungry. We opened the cabin door and met with an amazing sight.

Miss Sarah stood at our hearth, stirring the stew pot. Ma was still in bed, propped up by pillows, a mug of tea in her hands. Her eyes were red and swollen, but she smiled at us and held out her arms. She kissed us each in turn. "Poor girls," she said. "Can you remember your gran?"

Hezzy sat on the chair, which had been pulled to the side of the bed. In a low voice, she began telling Ma all the things she could remember. Ma nodded, crying a little but smiling too. Nan, who could not remember Gran at all, curled up by Ma's feet and listened.

At the hearth Miss Sarah dragged the Dutch oven off its pile of coals. "I'll do that," I said, moving to her side. She was wearing her sky-blue gown, with its ribbons and lace, and Ma's apron was not broad enough to cover it.

She smiled. "Go to your mother, Elizabeth."

No one ever called me Elizabeth. I made a face. I went to Ma and said, "I remember her red quilt."

"Aye," Ma said, "her album quilt. 'Twas beautiful."

"And her currant buns," I added.

Ma traced her finger along my cheek. "But do you remember her?" she asked. "Herself, not just the things she made."

I thought for a moment. "I remember that she smelled like flour," I said. "And that her skin was soft and smooth, like dough. And when she saw me, she would say, 'Here's my little Lizzy-loo!' "

Ma nodded, tears in her eyes. "You remember."

"I do," I said, and walked back to the fire. Would my family remember me so well, years hence? I had not had time to accomplish much.

Miss Sarah smiled at me but waved me away. "Truthfully I can cook," she said. "You need not worry. I will not scorch the stew."

I set the table, thumping the plates down hard. No one seemed to notice. For all Hezzy seemed to think that the sun rose and set on fine ladies from Charleston, she paid no mind to Miss Sarah now.

"I came the moment I heard," Miss Sarah said to me in an undertone. "I knew how your mother must feel. I lost my mother too, when I was but a girl."

I did not want to hear about anyone else dying. I climbed onto the seat of the loom. The baby's new blanket was almost done. Soon we would be starting Miss Sarah's coverlet. I picked up the shuttle and started to weave. *Clack-clack-thump. Clack-clack-thump.* I was not as good a weaver as Hezzy or Ma, but I was good enough. *Clack-clack-thump.* It felt comforting to watch the new fabric grow, to think of the new baby growing in Ma's belly. *Clack-clack-thump.* I threw the beater bar back as hard as I could. *Clack-clack. Thump.*

"Lizzy," Ma said softly, "come to the table now."

They were all sitting down for supper. Nan looked at me strangely. Miss Sarah sat on the end of the bench, between Hezzy and Pa. I sat across from her, next to Nan. The stew smelled delicious, and my stomach rumbled.

Pa glanced uneasily at Miss Sarah. "Take the blessing, ma'am," he offered.

Miss Sarah bowed her head. I kept mine up and watched her. "For our fellowship and food, for our loved ones far and near, for those who have gone to

You and those still awaiting Your glory, Lord, we are humbly grateful."

Ma sniffed into her handkerchief. Miss Sarah looked up at her, and they exchanged a gentle look. Despite Miss Sarah's finery, she and Ma had become friends.

CHAPTER THIRTEEN

After that Ma's belly pained her for some long time. 'Twas too early for the baby to safely arrive. Pa fetched Ma Silver, who stayed three days with us. Ma Silver said that our ma would be fine, so long as she kept to bed.

"Don't worry," Ma Silver said the first night, squatting crosswise on the hearth and lighting her pipe from an ember. "You're worried, ain't you?"

It took me a moment to realize she was speaking directly to me. I was standing at the table, making a dye pot for the wool for Miss Sarah's coverlet. Hezzy was spinning, fast as she could, while Nan carded still more wool. Hezzy had finished weaving the baby's blanket, but Ma told us to leave it on the loom until the pieces of Miss Sarah's coverlet were also done. We had enough warp, we thought. The three of us were working hard. We had a mind to finish the coverlet even if Ma could not weave.

"Yes, ma'am," I whispered to Ma Silver. Sometimes fear covered me like a net. Sometimes it felt like a stone I carried inside. Wherever I went, fear went with me. When I woke up in the morning it woke too, and it seemed to stay awake long into the night. I did not sleep well. Some days I could hardly work for my hands trembling.

"You're fussing too much," Ma Silver said. "Your ma'll be fine, but we'll be after callin' you Long-face Lizzy, the way you've been moping about this house. Did you ever hear me tell about the girl from up yonder, who worried too much?"

"No, ma'am," I whispered, more quietly than before, because I was not interested in hearing such a story. The worst thing was not being able to tell my family about my fear. It shamed me to be more worried about myself than about Ma and the baby, and Ma was already so grieved that the baby might be harmed. I could not add to her sorrow.

"Tell us," Nan piped up.

Ma Silver pulled her skirts out of reach of the fire. She leaned back against the table leg. She took a long pull on her pipe and began. "Once 'pon a time, 'twas a girl from up Jonesborough way, and the very moment she was born she commenced to worry. She worried whether her folks was going to feed her or not."

"That's silly," Nan said. She set her carders down and rested her chin in her hands. "Everybody feeds their babies."

Hezzy took her foot off the spinning wheel treadle just long enough to kick Nan in the shin. Nan made a face but went back to work. Ma Silver continued.

"You're right, 'twas silly indeed. Everybody on this earth feeds their babies, so long as they've got any food at all. Even so, this girl, she was a worryin'. And when she figured out that she was going to get fed regular, she started worryin' that she wasn't going to be kept warm. Winter came, and she was warm enough. Summer came, and she was warmer still.

"So she growed up, every year, worryin', every year, things coming out mostly fine. She worried folks didn't love her, but they did. She worried she wasn't pretty enough, but she was. Worried she wouldn't ever catch a man—but she did. She had five fine children, and from the moment the first was born she could hardly catch her breath, she was worryin' over them so."

Ma Silver puffed her pipe. She smiled at us.

"So what happened?" Hezzy prompted.

"Nothin'," Ma Silver said. "She lived to be eighty-four, died in her sleep with her family around her."

My hands shook a bit as I measured out the dye. 'Twas not fair to tell such a story about me. I was not worried about small things.

"That doesn't make sense," Nan complained.

"Sure enough it doesn't," Ma Silver said. "That girl, she spent her whole life feelin' unhappy when things were turning out just fine. What say you, Long-face Lizzy?"

What could I say? I waited for Hezzy, for Nan, for someone to realize what was wrong. When they did not, my hands began to tremble from anger, not fear.

"I think it's a stupid story," I said. I went outside and hung the dye pot over the big outdoor fire. I added more wood and sat watching the flames. The sun faded and the sky turned blue black. Nan came out with a lantern and an armful of skeined wool. I dipped the skeins into the indigo dye, one by one, over and over, bringing them up into the air until gradually they turned as blue black as the sky. As blue black as my heart.

CHAPTER FOURTEEN

One day the next week, I went to Suzy Pearlette's house to spend the afternoon. I took a drop spindle with me so that I could spin as I walked there. 'Twere two miles to the Pearlettes' farm.

Suzy was surprised and happy to see me. We walked up to the top of the hill in their sheep meadow and sat down in the tall brown grass. Suzy pulled up pieces of grass and made thumb-whistles. I pulled the wooden horse Charlie Smithson had made me out of my pocket and galloped it across my knee. I carried it with me, like a talisman, though it did not keep me from being afraid.

"Is Charlie still sweet on Hezzy?" Suzy asked.

"Aye," I said. "Yesterday he left her a posy by the door." Suzy smiled. "He's not so clumsy," I said. "He is getting better. Ma says he is growing into his feet."

"He'll have to grow a lot before he catches Mr. William," said Suzy.

"Aye," I admitted. I stroked the back of the little horse. "Suzy," I said hesitantly, "do you ever wish to read?"

Suzy lay back in the grass. A few of the sheep ventured near. "No," she said. She giggled. "What a silly question! What would I read if I could?"

'Twas true enough. "We have one letter," I said. "You could practice on that." I smiled. "Miss Sarah's Daniel can read," I said.

"Well, some folk can," said Suzy.

"But Hezzy wants to, now," I said. "She never did before. She's got this thing, inside her like, burning her up. She watched Mr. William the whole time last week at church—"

"Aye," cut in Suzy, "I noticed."

"—she watched Miss Sarah yesterday when she came to call, and then she tried to sit like her, and talk like her, and when Miss Sarah left, Hezzy said, 'Think, she knows so much, think all the words she can read.'"

It bothered me, the changes I saw in my sister. "'Tis all she thinks of. She doesn't notice what goes on around her." Like me, I thought but did not say.

"Hezzy was like that before Miss Sarah came," Suzy observed. "She always had an eye to her betters."

"She's worse now. And wanting to read."

"Aye, well, no one understands why your family's taken up with those Beaumonts," Suzy said. "Folks got to observe their station in life. Those Beaumonts ain't much like us."

"We have not taken up with them," I said. "They're our neighbors, that's all. Besides, Miss Sarah's not so different from my ma, or yours. She can cook stew."

"In a silk dress!" said Suzy. "Don't get in a tizzy. 'Tis no harm. They'll go home soon enough."

But I was in a tizzy, angry at Suzy, angry at the world. Fear was sitting on my chest, holding me against the grass. "Suzy?" I said quietly, anger seeping out around my words. "I'm going to die soon enough. That's my station in life."

Suzy frowned. "You are not," she said. "Don't say such a thing!"

"I am. I know I am."

She sat up and shook her skirt out angrily. "You are not. If you're going to say such a thing, you can just go home."

I was stung. "I'll go then," I said.

"Fine. Go."

I WALKED HOME quickly, angrily, spinning fast as I went. I let the thread run too fine. It snapped, and the spindle dropped into the dirt. I picked it up and threw it as far as I could. Then I had to search in the weeds to find it. When I reached the cabin, muddy and cross, Hezzy was sitting on the step with her flute. Mr. William sat beside her. So now Mr. William was visiting us too.

"Listen, Lizzy," Hezzy said, her voice gay, "Mr. William is teaching me a Charleston tune."

"I prefer Southwest Territory tunes," I said. "They are good enough for me."

In the cabin, Ma and Miss Sarah sat drinking tea. They smiled at me. I put my spindle and wool in my basket and stormed outside. I could not think what to do. Spinning was too quiet, too contained. I took Pa's ax and split firewood for an hour. Afterward my chest hurt, but my heart felt better.

CHAPTER FIFTEEN

The next Sunday we must have been more tired than usual. We all slept until full daylight, and when the church bells began to ring we were still half-ready, half-breakfasted, half-dressed. We hurried ourselves, but the service was started before we arrived.

Pa and Ma led the way to our pew. Hezzy followed, her hands folded demurely in front of her, her shoulders rounded because she was ashamed to be late. From the back pew Mr. William looked up at her as she went past. Hezzy did not look back at him.

Miss Sarah sat beside Mr. William, and on her other side sat a finely dressed older man. I knew he had to be Mr. Beaumont, young Mr. William's father, though I had never seen him before.

The preacher kindly stopped his sermon and let us

get settled before continuing. He stood at the pulpit, and when we had sat down he repeated his text again so we should know it. " 'The wages of sin,' " he said, " 'is death.' "

I had had a headache all morning. The preacher's words struck me like a hammer blow. "When we die we are destroyed," he said. I began to tremble as a leaf in a storm. "When we die we face eternal damnation." I stood up. My body swayed. The preacher did not notice me. He was preaching vigorously, his body bent with the force of his words, his eyes on the faithful in the back pews. "We die to be consumed by everlasting hell!"

A thin, watery wail, like a baby's cry, started in the back of my throat. I clutched at the back of the pew in front of me, braced myself, and screamed and screamed and screamed.

Pa grabbed me up. He carted me out of the church, down the steps, and away past the horse shed. The scream died out of me. I shivered.

Pa sat me on the ground beneath a walnut tree. He stood up and raised his hand to the people flocked around the church door. Then he turned his back on them and sat beside me. I watched them slowly drift back into the church, Ma and the preacher included.

When they were gone Pa smiled. "Ye didn't give him a chance to get to the good stuff," he said. "Ye got stuck on damnation. Ye know he'd be preaching salvation by the end."

I wiped my eyes, which were full of tears. Pa put his arm around me, and I leaned into his waistcoat. It smelled of tobacco. "I'm not going back to church," I said. "Not ever."

"Aye, well," Pa said, "I'll stay home with you."

I had expected him to fuss at me, and when he did not I cried. I was not noisy about it. I dried my face with my kerchief when I had done.

"I don't fear damnation," I said.

"Most Christians should," Pa said mildly.

"I fear dying," I said. "Sometimes I am so afraid."

Pa rubbed his thumb hard on the sore place between my shoulders. "Aye, lass," he said. "I fear it for you."

PA CARRIED ME home before the congregation was let out. We did not need, he said, to make more of a spectacle. Ma was anxious not to find us outside. She hurried home faster than she should have and gave Pa a tongue-lashing for leaving the church without telling her. Pa stayed inside to deal with her. I walked out to the apple trees. Hezzy followed me.

"We all know it," Hezzy said. "Maybe not Nan. Not Nan. But the rest of us do."

"Why didn't you speak of it?" I said. I hunched my shoulders and turned away from her. I whispered, "'Twould have helped me not to feel so alone."

Hezzy put her arms around me. "You are never alone," she said. "Think you of that long, cold night."

I kicked my bare foot on a root. "I'll be alone at the end," I said.

Hezzy's eyes swam with tears. "Not until then," she said.

"Oh, aye," I said. Some sort of meanness still swam in my breast. "And you after sweet William, and Ma with Miss Sarah, and then Charlie around to sop up the rest of your attention—there's so much left for me!"

"Lizzy!" Hezzy's face turned pink. I knew I should not say such things, but I was too sore and afraid not to. 'Twas safest to hurt Hezzy, after all. Hezzy was strong.

"I won't mind Mr. William," she said. "I'll stay with you."

"He's too fine for us, anyhow," I said.

Hezzy sighed. "I know that. I know."

AFTER THAT, I let myself curl up into a little ball. I became like a field mouse, small and frightened. I did not go to church. I did not visit Suzy Pearlette. When neighbors came to call I sat close by the fire, spinning, and barely spoke. Hezzy, Ma, and Pa were all soft to me, and Nan waited on me as though I were already an invalid.

I could feel my heart beating strong. I could feel my lungs breathing as they should. But I was so fearful that the rest of me felt sick anyway. I did not go out. I stayed by the fire, spinning, spinning, while Ma watched me with worried eyes, while Hezzy turned a blind face even to Mr. William and stayed with me, while even Pa fell silent. We were all waiting, watching; doom lay over us.

'Twas not the way we should be. I knew this.

THEN ONE DAY Ma Silver came to call. Hezzy, Nan, and Pa were all harvesting. Ma was visiting Mrs. Cole. I was spinning wool. I made Ma Silver a pot of tea, and then I resumed my work. Ma Silver sat by the fire, eyes half shut, smoking her pipe. Suddenly she opened one eye wide and said to me, "Are you well or aren't you?"

I had carded a full basket of wool so I could spin for a long time without interruption. I let two rolags play themselves into yarn before I answered. "I don't know."

Ma Silver shut her eyes and drew on her pipe. "Course you do."

"I'm going to die next fall," I said, so softly I could hardly hear myself.

Ma Silver opened her eyes. She gave me a long quiet look. "What are you going to do about it?" she asked.

"I can't do anything about it," I said. I felt a wave of panic and I swallowed hard. "There's nothing I can do."

Ma Silver raised herself up from the ground. She waddled over to the bench across from my stool and squatted down in front of me. One of her huge hands cupped my chin. "Don't worry about dying," she said. "What are you going to do with this time you have left?"

I didn't know what she meant. I didn't know how to answer. Her eyes looked into mine until I felt like a worm on a hook. I looked down at the wool in my hands. "Spin," I said. "Right now I'm going to spin."

Ma Silver smiled. "Good," she said. "Because you have two choices now. You can be afraid of everything, or you can be afraid of nothing at all."

CHAPTER SIXTEEN

You can be afraid of everything, or you can be afraid of nothing at all. I took my foot off the treadle, and the wheel gradually stopped. I looked at Ma Silver. She looked back at me.

It seemed suddenly so clear. Afraid of everything, or afraid of nothing. Because I would die anyhow, I knew that. Everyone knew it. But I had a choice.

I stood up. A great grin spread across my face. The wool dropped from my hands. Ma Silver smiled. I got up and threw my arms around her, laughing and then crying a little. She set me on her knee and wiped my face with the sleeve of her shift. " 'Tis a hard choice," she said. "Most grown folks can't face it, let alone a slip of a lass like you. You're a good'un, Lizzy, a fine brave girl."

A fine brave girl. Afraid of nothing at all. 'Twas true. With my fear lifted off me, I felt light as a bird wing, strong, courageous. "I suppose I'll go help with the harvest," I said.

"Thought you were going to spin," Ma Silver said. I looked at the wheel. "So I was," I said.

I made dinner first, a meat stew and sweet potatoes, a spider cake and applesauce. I brewed more tea and cleaned the cabin. Then I sat and spun and spun, soft wool, light as clouds. Ma Silver got on her pony and went home. When my family came in, I greeted them with laughter, and from the way Nan's face lit into a smile, and the way Pa's eyes twinkled over his mouthfuls of stew, I saw that they understood me, a little at least.

NOW THERE WERE many things I had to do. There was the harvest first, of course, and all the work that this busy time of year entailed. Our first quick frost had been followed by warmer weather, and so our work was following close to its usual pattern. There was the new baby to prepare for. And there was the matter of Hezzy.

"Why do you wish to read and write?" I asked her as we bent and stood in the field, shucking the corn Pa had cut. "What will it gain you?"

Hezzy stuffed a loose curl back into her mobcap. She wiped her face with her hand and frowned. "What will it not?" she said. "We could read our own letters then. We could write them."

I worked for a while, considering. The folks from Pennsylvania, scattered now, were so far away that they no longer seemed real to me. "You could ask Mr. William to teach you," I said at last, though I was not sure Hezzy should be so bold.

Hezzy made a face. "I never could," she said.

"'Tis true," I agreed. "Might be unseemly."

"And he would know," Hezzy said.

"Know what?"

"That I can't read. That none of us can."

I laughed. "He must know that, Hezzy. Gracious."

"He's not like us," Hezzy said. "He grew up so different. Miss Sarah—everyone where he comes from, seems like, knows so much more than we do. I don't want him to know, Lizzy. I don't want him to think me ignorant."

I could not think of words to say. Mr. William and Miss Sarah were as different from us as a fine trotting horse is from a mule. I did not think that shamed us. A mule, after all, was more useful. Miss Sarah could not weave her own coverlet, and I doubted very much if Mr. William or his fine father could cut oats so well as Pa.

"He said I was pretty," Hezzy whispered.

"Oh, Hezzy," I said.

"He did," Hezzy said. "He said my eyes were like stars."

'Twas foolishness, I could see. 'Twould do more harm than good.

And yet Hezzy *was* pretty. Her eyes *were* like stars.

WE FILLED our little loft with pumpkins and potatoes. We shelled enough beans to fill two sacks. We dried the last apples from our trees, and in the barn Pa threshed the oats and wheat and corn. We had food enough, and more.

Ma wove Miss Sarah's coverlet as fast as possible. We cut it and the baby's blanket from the loom. Nan sewed the ends of the blanket in, and Hezzy and I finished the coverlet. Miss Sarah paid Ma in coin. Pa took the money to Jonesborough when he went to trade for sugar and tea, but he did not find a sow that pleased him. He brought the coins back, and Ma put them in a pot on the mantelpiece. In the spring we would find a good pig.

Finally Ma shrouded the loom in an old cloth. "We'll rest now for a while," she said. Her belly had grown. She needed rest.

I WENT BACK to church. I sat quietly in my place and shut my ears against the preacher's words. I would not listen. Before and after services, I talked with Suzy Pearlette.

"What made you—" she started to say.

"Aye, I felt so ill that day," I said. "I thought 'twas my sickness again."

Suzy eyed me worriedly. "You look fine," she said.

"And so I am." I smiled. "Don't worry, Suzy. I'll not speak of dying." She grinned.

FROM THE PULPIT the minister announced an end-of-harvest celebration, a picnic dinner the Saturday hence. We had such a celebration every year, and though the minister did not say dancing I knew there would be, music and singing and dancing all into the night, and food and joyousness. After the service Hezzy went boldly to Mr. William and spoke with him before skipping over to Suzy and me. "He says he'll come, Lizzy! He says he wouldn't miss it for the world!"

Charlie Smithson was coming down the steps of the church. I looked over Hezzy's shoulder and saw him watching her. I saw something like a shadow pass across his face when he heard Hezzy's words. I wished my sister would curb her happiness. I wished she would think more of Charlie.

Then, as I looked at Charlie, my heart did a funny thing. Suddenly I wished he would think more of me.

CHAPTER SEVENTEEN

Hezzy asked Daniel to teach her to read.

I went with her to the Beaumonts' cabin. Hezzy had made a pretty excuse, to visit Miss Sarah with some fresh apple cake. She had a secretive light in her eyes that I thought meant Mr. William. I did not like it, so I asked Ma if I might walk along.

Hezzy gave me a sour look. Ma saw that and did not like it, so she gave me permission to go. Hezzy flounced her skirts and walked fast through the brown grass. I ran to keep up with her until my chest started to tighten. "Hezzy—please."

Hezzy slowed. She turned to me with her lips set in a line. "You keep your mouth shut about what I do," she said.

"If 'tis about Mr. William—"

" 'Tis not about Mr. William!" Hezzy walked faster before thinking of me again and slowing down. "The Beaumonts are going to Jonesborough today, so Mr. William said. All of them."

"So the apple cake—"

"Is for Daniel. For a reading lesson."

"Ah." I understood.

Inside the Beaumonts' cabin, Daniel and the cook were sitting on benches by the fire. Warm savory smells came from the pots on the hearth. When she saw us, Cook stood up, but Daniel stayed where he was. He bobbed his head at us, politely but slowly.

Hezzy laid the apple cake down on the table. She told Daniel why she had come. Daniel smiled slowly and quietly.

"No, miss," he said.

"But I'll pay you," Hezzy protested. "Something nice, every time. This cake. Something else—"

"No, miss," Daniel said again.

"But—" Hezzy looked dumbfounded. Cook glanced over her shoulder at Daniel. Something in her look made me understand. Daniel's refusal wasn't about Hezzy, or about reading. 'Twas that he had so few chances to say no.

"Leave be, Hezzy," I said quietly.

"But—" She raised her voice.

"Leave be."

Hezzy looked at me and sighed in exasperation. "Keep the cake, then," she said, and flounced out the door. I looked back as I followed her out. Cook was already drawing a knife across the top of the cake. Daniel gave me another slow grin.

"DON'T YOU EVER want to better yourself?" Hezzy asked me on the way home. "Don't you wish to know more?"

"Knowing more wouldn't make me better," I said.

"It could," Hezzy said. "If you read—the Bible! If you could read the Bible, like the minister but every day, you would be better and know more."

"Aye," I said slowly, because I could see the truth in that. In fact, I could see that some good might come of reading. "But is it really the reading that you want? The Bible and all?"

Hezzy glared at me. "Aye, of course," she said.

"Because knowing how to read will not make you like the Beaumonts," I said. "And being like them would not make you better. Wearing silk dresses and living in Charleston would not make you better."

Hezzy scowled and would talk to me no more.

CHAPTER EIGHTEEN

The morning of the church dinner, Hezzy could not be pleased. She fussed over her petticoat and asked to borrow mine. I gave it readily. Then she gave it back to me.

" 'Tis too short," she said.

"Aye, Hezzy, I am shorter than you," I said.

Nan giggled. Hezzy rubbed a spot on her bodice. She poked a lock of hair back into her cap. She picked up Pa's small shaving mirror and tried to see her whole self in it.

"Hezzy," Ma warned, "do not be vain."

Pa grinned. He seemed to be enjoying Hezzy. "The lads will look to your pretty face and not so much as see your clothes," he said. Hezzy turned pink and put the mirror away.

As OUR WAGON drew near the church, the merry sounds of a fife and fiddle sailed across the grass to greet us. Hezzy stood in the wagon bed, brushing wisps of hay from her petticoat. Pa stopped the horses, and Hezzy nearly fell down. She looked at Pa, and she giggled.

'Twas impossible to stay cross with Hezzy.

We climbed out of the wagon. Pa held Ma carefully as she came down. "I'm not made of china, now," she told him. Hezzy smoothed her skirts all around and pushed her hair back. She looked at Ma, smiling, hesitating. "Go on," Ma told her. Hezzy nodded and skipped off.

Nan and I unloaded our baskets from the wagon. Pa drove off to the shed. Nan and I and Ma walked laden to the trestle tables and set out our food. The tables were loaded. Just behind the church, too, a pig roasted over a fire pit. Boys took turns with the spit. The pig's skin sizzled. The air smelled smoky and meaty and good.

Nan stood next to me. "Biscuits!" she said. "Three kinds! And yeast bread! And jam!" Her stomach rumbled, loud enough for me to hear.

The music piped up louder in a bright dancing tune. People had taken the benches out of the church and put them on the grass in a rough half circle. In the middle, folks were gathering for a country dance. I saw Hezzy standing to one side, her hands relaxed against her skirt, her smile calm, waiting. She looked like a grown woman, not a child.

Hezzy's chin went up and her eyes began to shine. I looked in the direction she was looking just as Nan drew in her breath. Young Mr. William strode into the clearing. He was dressed more finely than we had ever seen him, even at church, even in the stagecoach that first day in Jonesborough. Gold braid glittered down the front of his jacket and around his cuffs, gilt buttons shone along his pantaloons, and even his silver shoe buckles glittered gold in the sun.

He walked toward Hezzy, who was waiting for him.

Nan looked at me and smiled. "Hezzy's golden boy," she said, with a little shake of her head.

I laughed. Who could blame Hezzy, after all, when he walked like a prince out of the woods and went straight to her side? And who could blame Mr. William for picking my bright sister out of the crowd? I grabbed Nan's hands and pulled her into the set.

"Come," I said, "come, let's dance."

LATER WHEN THE PORK was ready and Nan and I had filled our plates at the table, I saw Charlie Smithson sitting by himself on the grass. I went over to him, and Nan followed. We sat beside him and began to eat.

Nan said, "Isn't it wonderful?" She grinned at him.

"Oh, aye," he said glumly. He ate a piece of pork.

"We brought some of the sweet potatoes, and Lizzy made that apple pie." She pointed to a piece on Charlie's plate.

Charlie ate a bite and nodded at me. "'Tis very good," he said. 'Twas only to oblige me, I knew, but I liked his praise. The pork was crisp and juicy. All the food was wonderful good. The air was cool and clean smelling, and I felt dizzy from happiness. When I was finished eating, I took the wooden horse Charlie had made me out of my pocket and galloped it across my knee.

He smiled. "I wondered if you'd gotten that," he said. "You were so sick."

"Aye." Already it seemed long ago. The leaves on the trees were past their bright colors; they were turning brown. "I carry it with me," I said.

"I thought you would like a toy."

This was not what I hoped Charlie Smithson would say.

"Hezzy keeps dancing with Mr. William," Nan chirped. "I wonder if she'll even stop to eat."

Charlie scowled. He bent over his plate.

"He'll be gone in the spring," I said softly.

Charlie said nothing.

"Winter comes, there won't be much visiting," I said. "Then in the spring he'll be gone. When his father's business is done. He'll not come back here."

Charlie wiped his plate with a piece of bread. "Aye," he said softly.

"Hezzy is too young to be serious," I said quietly. I watched Charlie's hands, brown and strong.

"Aye," Nan said, puzzled by my words. "Why should she be serious today? This is fun."

Charlie looked up at her and grinned. "Aye, Miss Nan, will you dance with me, then?"

"Aye!" Nan sprang to her feet.

I sat for a moment on the brown grass, watching the figures and listening to the music. Then I gathered the plates and went to see how my mother fared. With her belly so large and round, she looked ready for harvest herself.

CHAPTER NINETEEN

When Miss Sarah next came to our cabin, she brought with her a basket of fancywork. She and Ma sipped tea and sewed together. Ma was mending the tiny shifts that Nan had worn, and before that Hezzy and me, to get them ready for the new babe. Miss Sarah was embroidering a piece of fine cotton cloth with bright silken thread.

'Twas the richest work I'd ever seen. The blue and gold silk shimmered as bright as sky and sunshine and followed Miss Sarah's needle through the smooth cloth like water running through a riverbank. When Miss Sarah saw me staring, she spread the piece flat on the table for all of us to see.

" 'Tis a pocket," she said, though anyone with eyes could tell that.

We all wore pockets around our waists. Ma, with so many bits and pieces to carry, wore two. But ours were made of scrap cloth, the leftovers from our bodices and shifts, and we wore them under our petticoats, out of sight. Miss Sarah would wear this beautiful pocket outside her skirts for everyone to admire.

Hezzy had been sitting near the fire, demure and good, her hands folded on her lap like a lady. When she saw the pocket she leaned forward. "Oh, Ma!" she said. "Couldn't we—couldn't I?" She paused. "I do need a new pocket," she said.

Ma said nothing, only looked at her. Miss Sarah gathered her pocket back into her hands, but she smiled at Hezzy in a friendly way. "When I have finished this one, I will make it a present to you," she said.

Hezzy gaped, then blushed. She understood how rude she had been. "Oh, no!" she said fiercely. "Truly I would not take it. I only meant—I only—'twould be a pleasure to make something so lovely, that is all."

Miss Sarah smiled again. Her hands seemed to relax a little. "Are you so fond of beauty, Hezzy?" she asked.

Hezzy nodded, a little reluctantly. "Aye," she said. "I'm fond of pretty dresses"—she looked at Ma— "and coverlets, and flowers, and words. Sometimes clouds or wind."

"Wind?" asked Miss Sarah.

"Aye, when it ripples through a wheat field, or tall grass. You can see it, up and down and up again."

Miss Sarah got a queer expression on her face. "It looks like ocean waves," she said.

"I would like to see the ocean," said Hezzy.

We were all quiet for a moment. Only Ma's fingers moved, driving her needle in and out around a rip on the baby's shift. I thought Hezzy's wishes showed too plainly in her voice. She would hurt Ma, wanting things she could not have. I wondered, for a moment, if I wished to see the ocean. I decided I did not. The wind through the wheat fields was enough for me.

"I like faces," I said, to break the odd silence. "Nan's face first thing in the morning, and Hezzy's, when she smiles."

"She has a beautiful face," Miss Sarah said softly. "I would wish for a daughter half so fair."

Hezzy's eyes lit like stars.

CHAPTER TWENTY

Ma banged pot lids after Miss Sarah left. She did not say that she was cross with Hezzy, but we knew she was. "I did not do anything wrong," Hezzy protested.

"Begging for a pocket," Nan murmured.

"I did not mean it that way!" Hezzy said. "Nan, you know I did not."

"Did so."

"Did not!"

"You didn't think you meant it," I said, interrupting them. "You didn't think about it first, but you meant it, you know you did. You spoke truly. You wanted that pocket."

Hezzy blushed. "I did not mean to say so. Ma, don't be angry."

Ma kept her face toward the fire, cooking. She did

not speak for a while. "You, daughter," she said at last, "do not be thinking yourself too high."

"I won't," Hezzy promised.

IN THE MORNINGS now 'twas frosty in the cabin. I often woke before the rest. I liked to lie still, cuddled betwixt Hezzy and Nan, and listen to the soft sounds of them breathing. The banked fire gave off faint heat. The wool coverlets felt soft and scratchy at the same time. As the early morning wore closer to dawn, the outlines of the windows grew sharper. Before the sun came up, Ma and Pa would wake.

Ma grew rounder and slower. Hezzy lifted the pots on the hearth for her. Nan and I fetched the buckets of water. We tried to spare her all the heavy work. Sometimes Ma Silver came to see how Ma did. She was there, drinking tea, when Miss Sarah next came.

There was only the one chair and Ma Silver was sitting in it. Miss Sarah sat down on a bench quite graciously. She set a small bundle wrapped in linen on the table. She called Hezzy over and unfolded it.

The linen gave way to a long piece of cotton cloth and a twist of crimson silk. I squeezed between Ma and Hezzy on the bench. I saw Ma's lips press into a fine line, saw happiness and doubt in Hezzy's eyes.

"I happened to have so much extra," Miss Sarah

said kindly. "I cannot see a use for it myself, Hezzy. Perhaps you could sew your own pocket? 'Twould be good practice with your needle." Miss Sarah gave a nod to Ma as she said the last bit.

"Hezzy sews a strong straight seam," Ma said.

"That's a lively color," Ma Silver said, stirring the silk with one fat finger. "Cost a pretty penny, that did."

Hezzy sat unmoving. I knew she wanted to make that pocket. I knew she worried what Ma would say.

"Let her," I whispered to Ma. "'Tis a small thing."

Ma looked at me. I bit my lip. Hezzy did so well, usually. She wanted fine things, but she was happy without them. And it was not very much silk, after all.

I thought these things but could not say them. It seemed that Ma understood, however, because she turned to Miss Sarah with a smile. "'Tis kindhearted of you," she said. "Hezzy, you will have to stitch carefully to deserve such a gift."

Hezzy's eyes shone but she did not smile. She slid the pile of cloth across the table and ran her hand over it. "Thank you, Miss Sarah," she said.

"You are welcome, Hezzy."

Nan crowded between Hezzy and me. "Let me see," she said. "Ooh, how pretty!" She held the cloth up to the light.

Miss Sarah creased her brow. "I did not think," she said. "I should have brought enough for you, Nan. For Lizzy, too. Enough to share."

Nan dropped the cloth quickly. "Oh, no," she said. "I don't like fancywork. My stitches are not fine enough for that."

Nan's sincerity was obvious, and it satisfied Miss Sarah. "Lizzy?" she asked softly, with a tilt of her head.

Hezzy had found a scrap of paper and was drawing flowers on it with a bit of charcoal, a pattern for her pocket, I guessed. She bit her lip in concentration. One curl curved over her brow.

I remembered another pattern Hezzy had drawn. "Thank you, no," I said to Miss Sarah. I turned to Ma. "What I want, please, is a fleece."

We had used several of our fleeces already, but Ma let me look over the ones that were left. I chose the largest.

"If you need more wool, take another," Ma said.

I folded the greasy fleece until it was a bundle I could carry in my arms. "I'll need flax, too," I said. Ma looked at me. I looked at her. "For the warp," I said.

"You'll be wanting the loom, then," she said.

"Aye."

From Ma's face I could see that she would give me

anything and everything she could. The use of the loom was easy. She did not ask questions. I was glad.

First I took the big iron pot and hung it over the outdoor fire. I put my wool into it and boiled it carefully, without stirring, so the fleece would not turn into felt. I spread the clean wool in the sun to dry.

Winter days were coming. Pa went hunting. The rest of us worked inside.

Hezzy planned for days before she touched a needle to the piece of cotton cloth that would be her pocket. She drew on bits of paper with a burnt stick, then shook her head and tried again. She unwound the twist of silk and tried to guess how much embroidery it would make. Miss Sarah watched her efforts with great interest, seeming not to notice Ma's scowls. Finally Hezzy settled on a light, airy, open pattern to work clear across the cloth.

She wished to begin it one afternoon. All morning we had been working with Ma, washing clothes and ironing them. No sooner had we sat down to our dinner than the daylight darkened. It was cold enough now that we had to keep the cabin door closed, but we had the windows unshuttered and sunlight filtered through the greased-paper panes. Suddenly that light was gone. Hezzy made a low noise in her throat, almost a growl.

"Nay, miss," Pa said, "I'll not be lighting candles for you to do fancywork by."

A flash of lightning and a crack of thunder stifled Hezzy's reply. We hastened to shutter the windows while drops of rain fell heavy on the roof. Inside the darkened cabin Pa stirred the fire. Thunder boomed again and rain fell in torrents.

Hezzy poured water into the washbasins and Nan and I began to clear the table. Suddenly Ma jumped up from the chair with a startled cry. A rush of water ran out from under her petticoats along the floor. At first I thought 'twas rain coming under the door, but 'twas not, it had come from Ma. She wrapped her arms around her great belly and groaned. Her groan turned into a laugh at the end.

"Fetch Ma Silver," she said to Pa. "The baby's coming now."

CHAPTER TWENTY-ONE

Pa clapped on his hat and his leather hunting shirt. He put his hands on Ma's shoulders before he left.

"Nay, go," she said, the laugh still in her voice. "'Twill be well enough. But hurry."

Pa took a lantern and went out into the rain. I watched him run to the stable. When he came out, leading one of our horses, a crack of lightning lit the sky. The horse put its ears back at the driving rain.

"Come, Lizzy," said Ma. "You'll be soaked through."

Ma sat at the table in Pa's chair. Every now and again she hugged her belly tight and groaned softly. Nan sat beside her, wide-eyed, while Hezzy and I hurried to clean the dishes and clear the food away.

"What next, Ma?" Hezzy asked when we had

done. The storm raged on. Now water was coming in around the door. It trickled across the floor to meet the puddle already under Ma's feet.

Ma's eyes sparkled. "I'll be telling you, and you'll be doing it," she said carefully. "Because I know one thing, and I know it well: this baby is not waiting for Ma Silver."

We froze. "'Tis coming now, Ma?" Nan asked timidly.

"Soon enough," Ma said. "Now, you will all do as I say."

We pushed the table against the loom and stuck the benches under it. We pulled the underbed out from the big bed and pushed it into the corner made by the table and the wall. Hezzy threw her cloak over her head and brought in enough wood to last us the night. She piled the wet logs around the fire, where they sizzled and steamed. Then Hezzy brought water.

Meanwhile, I built the fire up until the cabin walls seemed to glow. I hung our kettle and our soup pot over the flames. Ma said we would need warm water to wipe the babe with.

Nan held on to Ma while she undressed and put on an old mended shift. At Ma's direction, Nan took the new coverlet off the bed and got out a pile of old, clean linens. Then Ma lay resting, sweating some. Nan and I took turns rubbing her back.

"I could go for Miss Sarah," Hezzy said. "She's closest."

"Nay," Ma said. "She's never had a baby."

"Mrs. Hough, then," Hezzy said. "Mrs. Smithson."

"I'll go," I offered.

"Nay." Ma laid a hand on Hezzy's shoulder. "Nay, Hezzy. There is not much time. And I'd rather it be you."

I made mint tea. Rain lashed against the house. I expected the storm to blow through and be gone, but it did not. If anything, it grew stronger. Hezzy paced the floor while Ma lay on the bed with her eyes closed.

I sat on the underbed with my back against the wall. Nan sat beside me and reached for my hand. "'Tis a natural thing," I whispered. "Think of the sheep. They have their babies in the fields."

Nan shook her head. "I'm still scared."

I was not scared. I was not afraid of anything now. Even if I had been scared of some things, even if I still feared death, this wild, glorious day would not have had power over me. This small babe, too, what harm could it bring? We all of us rested in the hand of God.

Suddenly Ma half sat and braced herself against the side of the bed. "Hezzy," she said.

Hezzy shot me a look as she went to Ma. 'Twas a

fierce, proud look, and I knew by it that Hezzy too was not the least bit afraid.

HEZZY CAUGHT THE BABE, but I was the first to wrap her in soft cloths and carry her to the fire. Nan helped me wipe her down. Together we examined her tiny, skinny feet, her perfect, star-shaped hands. Dark hair stuck to her forehead. She wailed vigorously and kicked her legs. We wrapped her warmly and carried her back to Ma.

Ma put her to the breast, and the tiny babe, so new, began to suck. I knelt down beside the bed and watched them with awe.

Then the door flew open and slammed against the wall. Pa and Ma Silver bumped into each other in their rush to cross the threshold. Rain streamed everywhere.

Hezzy stood and met Pa squarely, hands on hips. "Aye, sir, you have another daughter," she said with a challenging toss of her head.

Ma Silver was already examining the babe. Pa looked Hezzy up and down. "Aye, then," he said in a voice to match Hezzy's, "if she's half the daughter you are, she'll be fine indeed."

Chapter Twenty-two

Ma and Pa named our new sister Martha, after Gran. We all called her Patsy from the start. She weighed less than a large hen, but Ma Silver and our ma both said she was a healthy baby, big and strong. She had dark eyes that seemed to look through people rather than at them. She rarely cried and could be easily soothed.

Ma Silver stayed with us only a few days. After that, Nan and Hezzy and I were proud that we could do everything for Ma. We cooked and cleaned and did the wash. We rocked Patsy for hours.

I had begun to pick apart and card the wool from my fleece. I found a way to card with my hands while rocking Patsy's cradle, steadily, with my feet. Patsy loved to rock.

Miss Sarah brought a baby gift, a pair of wee white baby stockings, knit of soft lamb's wool. I was surprised; I might have guessed she would bring something fancier and less useful. Hezzy picked them up and exclaimed, "How beautiful! Miss Sarah, did you knit these yourself?"

"Aye," Miss Sarah murmured. "I mean, yes, I did. We cannot have her wee feet cold this winter." She bent over Patsy's cradle as she spoke and stroked Patsy's cheek with her finger.

"Here," Nan said, scooping Patsy up and laying her in Miss Sarah's arms. "She likes for people to hold her."

"Oh," Miss Sarah said. "Oh, she's as light as a kitten, the little dear." Miss Sarah smiled, but in an instant her smile tightened. Her eyes looked sad. They filled with tears.

"Hezzy," Ma said quietly, "do you take your sister outside. 'Tis time for her to get a breath of air." To Miss Sarah she said, "Now. I'll make us both some tea."

'Twas a fine warm day for mid-December. Hezzy lifted Patsy off Miss Sarah's lap, wrapped her carefully in her blanket, and carried her out into the bright sunshine. I slid my feet into my shoes and followed.

Patsy was awake and her eyes were open. Her little cap covered her funny head, and her thick dark hair stuck out around the edge of it. Wisps of Hezzy's own thick hair curled around her forehead. When she held Patsy near her face, they looked much alike.

Hezzy cradled Patsy close and twirled around the yard. She hummed a tune under her breath. Her indigo petticoats swirled out, and her feet danced. Patsy was too young to smile, but she looked happy and surprised. Hezzy hummed and twirled.

I stood on the doorstep and slowly closed the door behind me. Charlie Smithson was coming out of the woods. When he saw Hezzy dancing with the baby, he stopped for a moment. A look came to his face of heartfelt longing. In an instant, he seemed a man grown.

"Good morning, Charlie!" Hezzy waved to him and held Patsy up. "Have you come to admire her? Isn't she pretty?"

Charlie pushed the edge of the blanket away from Patsy's face. "She's as pretty as I thought she'd be," he said. "As pretty as her sisters."

He stood very close to Hezzy. She looked up at him—*Gracious,* I thought, realizing that Charlie had grown tall—and her face turned slightly pink. Her eyes danced.

"Good day, Miss Hezzy, Miss Lizzy. Good day, Charles. Is this the perfect child?" Mr. William walked around the side of the cabin. I was so surprised, I could do no more than nod at him. Hezzy started, and Charlie stiffened.

'Twas impossible for them not to admire Hezzy. She was so bright and lovely. She came back to me and sat on the step, and both boys hovered over her, crowding me to one side. I knew that if I had been holding Patsy, they would not have stood so close.

Then Patsy made a small noise and vomited, as babies do, in a thin milky streak down Hezzy's short gown. Charlie and Mr. William both jumped back. I expected to see fine Mr. William turn away. Instead he pulled a lawn handkerchief from his pocket, wiped the corner of Patsy's little mouth, and handed the handkerchief to Hezzy to sop herself.

Patsy began to cry and Hezzy took her back inside. She invited both boys in. Mr. William went first. Charlie shook his head at me as he gave me a hand to stand. "I wish I carried a handkerchief," he said.

CHAPTER TWENTY-THREE

"Once upon a time."

Ma Silver raised her arms up high and dropped her voice down low. We all fell quiet, listening.

'Twas Christmas Eve. At midnight Pa would go out with the other men and fire his musket into the sky. On Christmas Day we would all go to church, and eat a wild turkey for our dinner. We planned no other celebration. But Ma Silver came by in late afternoon, to see how Patsy fared, she said.

Ma Silver had no family of her own. Pa asked her to stay to supper and she quickly agreed. She squatted by the fire and smoked her pipe. Ma made bean porridge and popped a kettle of corn. When we had finished eating, Ma Silver drained her tea and said she had a story to tell. She shifted closer to the fire.

"Once upon a time," she said, "the world was newer, emptier." Her voice deepened and became smooth. "Come nighttime, fires blazed on the hillsides to keep the animals and the men who watched them warm. Once upon a time, around those fires storytellers sat and told tales, from the memory of a thousand years ago, and of things still yet to come."

In the firelight Nan's hair gleamed red gold, and her eyes shone. Patsy, cradled on Hezzy's lap, made a soft peep. I went to the wheel and quietly started it, spinning my wool while Ma Silver spun her tale.

"Town folk slept in brick houses, under wool blankets"—she nodded toward me and my spinning—"but on the hill there was only the fires and the sheep.

"There was a king in that land then, who said to himself, 'How many subjects do I have?' He decided to count them. So he sent out word that all his people must go to the village where they had been born, no matter where they lived now. He wanted 'em counted in proper order.

"'Twas winter, a poor time for traveling, but he was king and he must be obeyed. So a man took his pregnant wife and put her on a donkey, and they walked for many days. The wife, still not but a child herself, did not complain. She weren't the type to complain.

"On those hillsides above Bethlehem, with those

sheep, the storytellers told of a new king to be born right there in that city—a king spoken of a thousand years before. On the streets of Bethlehem, men, women, and children looked for somewhere to sleep. The city was small and filled with people come to be counted.

"When this man and his pregnant wife arrived there were no beds for them, nor even space on a floor. Not anywhere, not in the whole town.

"But one innkeeper's wife was pregnant too. She felt sorry for that lass on the donkey. She showed them a cave on the edge of town, where the innkeeper kept his cows and some sheep. From the mouth of the cave they could see the shepherds' fires in the night.

"The woman had her baby in that cave that night. Seemed like the very sky burst open with fire and light. On the hill the shepherds threw themselves to the ground, and the storytellers shook hardest of all. Voices, sweet and terrifying, filled their ears, and afterward no one who'd heard them could remember or repeat what they'd said. But they knew a king had come.

"They ran down that hill to the dark cave. They expected a crowned king with armies around him.

"They found a suckling babe."

The fire crackled. Ma Silver reached forward and stroked Patsy's cheek.

"The innkeeper's wife cared for the young mother," she continued. "The mother tended her child. The father found work repairing travelers' carts and bought them food and cloth to swaddle the babe.

"The shepherds gave them soft wool to pad the rough manger where he lay.

"The father never did sign up to be counted. He was not put down as a subject of the king. Neither was the mother or the child.

"That was right. The baby was a king himself—a true king, a king over all the earth. Only the shepherds knew this, but they spread the word. The storytellers handed down the tale."

Ma Silver quit speaking and her hands fell back at her side. She leaned forward till her forehead almost touched Nan's. "We are all storytellers," she said as Nan's eyes grew wider. "We all must remember this tale and pass it down."

CHAPTER TWENTY-FOUR

"She made that story sound like the truth," Nan said when Ma Silver had left. From far away, we heard gunshots, our neighbors celebrating Christmas.

"'Twas the truth," Hezzy said. "That story's in the Bible, Nan, you know that."

"But she made it sound like a story, *and* the truth," Nan persisted.

"So?" said Hezzy.

"So 'twas wonderful," Nan said.

DURING THE COLD bright winter days following Christmas, Hezzy embroidered her pocket and I spun my wool. Nan learned to sew Pa a new shirt. Our cabin was cozy and we did not lack for visitors. Miss Sarah came often.

"I declare, it seems so lonesome here in wintertime!" she said one cloudy morning.

We looked at her. We did not know what she meant.

"In Charleston, we entertain in the winter," she explained. "We host parties, and we go to them."

Hezzy sighed happily. She set her needle into her fabric and edged closer to Miss Sarah. "Tell us about Charleston," she said.

Nan looked up over her shirt. "Tell us a story," she said. Since Christmas Nan wanted everything to be a story.

Miss Sarah smiled. " 'Tis on the ocean, Charleston, as you must know, and ships come every day, from all parts of the world," she said. "So the shops are filled with delicacies from all across the world. China tea, oranges, chocolate. Some of the streets are paved with brick. 'Tis warm there even in winter; it never snows. In winter we live in our house in town. In summer, when the city is hot and foul-smelling, we move to our plantation."

Miss Sarah shook her head playfully. "You must not imagine us to be part of the first circle of society!" she said. "Oh, no! Charleston has many finer folk. Our plantation is smaller than most; we have fewer Negroes and less land. My husband aspires to a larger place. 'Tis why we are here, of course, to make our fortune."

It amazed me to think that someone as rich as Miss Sarah could hope to be still richer. Hezzy said, "Why did you come here with him? You could have stayed there and gone to the parties. I would have."

"Hezzy," Ma said reprovingly.

"Nay, I wanted to come," Miss Sarah told her. "I wanted adventure, and I did not want to be so long parted from my husband. I do not mind being here, except for the quietness."

"Do you have lots of servants?" Nan asked. "In Charleston?"

"Aye," said Miss Sarah. "Not so many as some folk, but thirty or forty all told."

"Are they all slaves?" asked Nan.

"Most of them."

"Why?" asked Nan.

Hezzy raised her eyebrows at Nan. Nan leaned forward earnestly.

"That's how you run a plantation," Miss Sarah explained. "With slaves. We grow indigo and rice, crops that require much labor."

"You wouldn't make so much money then," Nan said, "if you had to pay regular wages."

"That's right," said Miss Sarah.

I could see where Nan was headed. I wondered Ma did not stop her.

"Why do you need more money?" asked Nan. "You have more than anyone else I know."

"Nan!" Hezzy said.

Nan said, "The minister says slavery is a sin."

Miss Sarah's eyes flashed. It was the first time I had seen her looking other than pleasant. "Which minister?" she asked.

"Ours," Nan said. "The one you go to of a Sunday."

"He doesn't say it often, then," Miss Sarah said. "He wouldn't say it at all, I daresay, if he was trying to run a plantation of his own."

Nan had a stubborn look. So did Miss Sarah. "What dyes your petticoat, child?" she asked. "Indigo, that's what. When did you last eat rice? Aye, besides"—here she sighed a bit—"women have no say in this world. We do our husbands' bidding. We cannot speak for ourselves."

"Aye, besides," Hezzy said, "you say yourself that 'tis these land dealings that will make your fortune, not your crops or slaves."

Miss Sarah brightened. "'Tis true, Hezzy! 'Twill be the land dealings that allow us to feed our slaves, and clothe and house them well. Folk must accept their station in life, Nan. Some are born gentry, and some are born slaves."

"And some," Ma said softly, "are born neither."

I thought she meant that as a reminder to Hezzy, but Miss Sarah nodded as though Ma was talking to her. "Aye," she said. She seemed happy to close the conversation. For a while she watched Hezzy stitch, and soon she went home.

When she was gone Hezzy scowled at Nan. "Miss Impertinence! You should not speak so to a guest!"

Nan scowled back. "Not to Miss Sarah, you mean. You'd—"

"Hezzy!" Ma said. "I need water before supper. Nan, fetch some wood for the fire." Still scowling, my sisters flounced out. I looked up from my spinning.

"Do you believe what she said, Ma?" I asked.

"What who said?" Ma asked. "I believe slavery is a sin, aye, I do." She folded up her sewing. "Though maybe 'twould be easier for me to believe different if I had money to buy a slave. I don't believe we need riches, no. I've not yet gone to bed hungry, nor too cold to sleep. What we have seems enough."

"But think you," I persisted, "that women have no say?"

Ma grinned. "Nan had her say, did she not?"

CHAPTER TWENTY-FIVE

What followed was a set of days calm, unchanging, and precious to me. The weather continued cold and dull, but our hearth was bright and our friends visited often. Pa mended fences, threshed grain, hackled the flax. Patsy grew fat and stayed happy. Hezzy did her daily work without complaint. Mr. William came, sometimes with Miss Sarah on her visits, and sometimes on his own; Charlie came likewise, both with and without his mother. Nan, I noticed, had a sharper look to her. She was more often watching all of us, and less often in a world of her own dreams.

I paid attention to everything. Patsy's sweet baby smell, the smooth taste of hot tea, the sound of Ma's laughter: each day was full of treasures. When I wasn't eating, or sleeping, or cradling Patsy, I spun and spun the wool from my fleece.

"I can help you," Nan offered.

I shook my head. "'Tis my own," I said. "My one own thing."

Nan pursed her lips. "I can help you dye the wool. I can help wind the skeins."

"True enough," I said. "You can fill the bobbins, too, when it comes to that." Ma was warping the loom for me now.

"Will you be making the wool blue?" Nan asked. She looked at the ground. "Will you be using indigo?"

"Oh, Nan." For a moment I didn't know what to say. "Indigo is the best dye. I need two colors for the pattern. Indigo is dark and pretty. It stays fast in the wash, and it doesn't fade much."

Nan looked unhappy. "I cannot stop slavery by not using indigo," I said. "Nan, you know I cannot. I cannot do anything to help."

Nan sighed. "Walnut hulls," she said.

"They make brown! 'Twould be ugly, well you know it too."

"Pokeberry," Nan said.

"Aye, if I want my wool to fade back to white by next summer." I was starting to feel angry. I understood how Nan felt, but she asked too much. "I want my coverlet to last," I said. "For years and years. Forever."

"'Tis a coverlet you're making, then?" said Nan. "You've said naught about it."

"Aye."

Hezzy looked up from her embroidery. "Make it soft colors," she said. "Not white and blue. Make darker yellow and lighter yellow, or darker brown and lighter brown. 'Twould be pretty." She smiled at both of us.

"If it pleases you, Hezzy," I said. I could see as soon as Hezzy spoke that it would be pretty, a soft coverlet of soft colors, woven together like the colors in a field of grass. I smiled at Nan. "If it pleases you both, it pleases me."

Nan smiled. "I'll mix the dye pots," she offered. "I don't mind."

LATER THAT WEEK we heard word that Miss Sarah was ill. A bit of snow had fallen, and we all of us except Pa tramped through it on our way to Miss Sarah's cabin. Smoke rose out of the chimney, and the glass window sparkled.

Ma held Patsy tight against her chest, well wrapped, beneath her cloak. I carried a loaf of corn bread, and Hezzy a pail of stew. 'Twas silly of us—we forgot Miss Sarah had a cook. When we arrived Mr. William and Mr. Beaumont, Miss Sarah's husband, were sitting down to a meal much finer than the one we had brought. Hezzy flushed a bit.

"Welcome," Mr. Beaumont said, standing up as we came in. He bowed to Ma and nodded to the rest of us. Miss Sarah spoke a soft greeting from her bed in the corner. Hezzy handed her stew to me and went to Miss Sarah's side. The rest of us stood before Mr. Beaumont.

I hardly knew him at all. I saw him in church some weeks, when he was not away speculating. Mostly I knew of him from what Miss Sarah said, that he kept slaves and was bent to make his fortune, to be part of fine society. Now he looked at Ma and smiled kindly. I had expected a prouder man.

"We brought some food for by-and-by," Ma said. She put the stew and corn bread on the table. Ma looked, in this cozy cabin, the equal of anybody.

Mr. Beaumont gravely thanked her. "It smells wonderful," he said. "Indeed, we shall have some now." He took a spoon and ladled some onto his plate, and Mr. William's, next to their ham and meat pie. "Get a plate for Miss Sarah," he said abruptly. The Negro cook, whom I had heard called only Cook, came out of the corner. She fixed a plate for Miss Sarah and carried it to her.

I had not realized she was standing there until Mr. Beaumont spoke to her. That was how slavery worked, I supposed: through not seeing a person as a person. Or maybe 'twas the other way, that a person who was a slave learned to fade into the background.

"You must be Lizzy," Mr. Beaumont said to me. I nodded, and he smiled. "And here is Nan," he said, chucking her under the chin, "and of course that must be Hezzy, of whom I have heard so much." He nodded across the room. "And madam, you must let me see the babe."

Ma smiled at Mr. Beaumont. "Perhaps you would let Lizzy show you our Patsy," she said, "while I see what Miss Sarah needs." Mr. Beaumont bowed to her, smiling, so I took Patsy and unwrapped her close to the fire while Ma joined Hezzy at Miss Sarah's side. Mr. Beaumont looked at Patsy with interest and said many fine things about her. He even held her a moment.

In the corner, Ma was helping Miss Sarah change her shift while Hezzy plumped the bedclothes. Mr. William sat at the table, eating; when he saw me looking at him he winked. Every so often he glanced at Hezzy, but Hezzy was pretending not to see him at all. Only when Ma took our leave and Hezzy rose to join us did a small smile play quickly over her face.

She cast her eyes demurely down. Mr. William all but stared at her.

"Miss Sarah is none so poorly," Ma said as we walked home. "She has a slight catarrh and a fever. I told her to send Mr. William to Ma Silver for some herbs."

MISS SARAH, so we heard, improved greatly in a few days. But I took sick with the same illness, and 'twas not long before my life was again despaired of.

CHAPTER TWENTY-SIX

The sickness began simply enough. My cheeks grew hot, though I felt cold. I coughed, and phlegm rose in my throat. I was tired. My arms and legs ached.

Ma covered me warmly and fed me broth. "'Tis the same as Miss Sarah," Ma said, "and she is not so poorly. You'll be better soon." I smiled at her and drifted into sleep.

By morning I could not breathe. 'Twas the same feeling as I had had before harvesttime: my sides hurt as though a band were tight around them, and each breath I drew pained me. My eyes did not itch and my nose did not run, but oh, I could barely breathe. Ma, when she saw me, could not hide her anxiousness, and Hezzy and Nan looked wide-eyed. Pa went for Ma Silver before breakfast.

"Set her up, set her up," Ma Silver said. "Boil some water for tea, eh? Up with ye, Lizzy, don't be lyin' down!" She propped me in the chair and rubbed my back. "How bad is it?" she asked.

"Bad," I whispered between gasps.

"Aye, then." She stopped rubbing and looked hard at me. "We'll do all we can. It worked before. Might not now. You know that, don't you?"

Hezzy put her hands on my shoulders. Nan crowded next to Ma Silver and squeezed my hand. "I know," I said. I could hardly speak, and my words came between gasps. "I'm . . . not . . . afraid."

Ma Silver nodded. "That's right. We'll do our best."

"Me—me too."

THAT AFTERNOON our cabin filled with the sound of waiting. Ma, Pa, and my sisters did not so much as step outside. Neither did they speak. They made me teas and poultices, and then they sat looking at me. Pa stroked my hand. Patsy nursed and cried and slept.

"Don't stare at me," I whispered.

" 'Tis not staring," Ma said. "We are watching you, is all."

I worked at breathing for several minutes, until I could speak again. "My coverlet," I said. "I wished to weave it—myself."

Hezzy's eyes filled with tears. "I'll weave it," she said. "Nan and I both."

Nan pushed my hair back from my face. "I am going to be a storyteller," she said. "Like Ma Silver. I have decided."

I nodded to show I had heard her.

"I will tell your story," she said. "Patsy will know all of her sisters."

At that tears ran down my own cheeks. I was still not afraid of dying. But yet I longed to live.

As THE CABIN grew dark that night Mrs. Smithson arrived. "Ma Silver stopped by, said you folks could use help," she said. She unloaded a basket full of food, brewed tea for me, and made Ma eat and drink and go to sleep. "You're nursing that baby," she said, tucking Patsy beside Ma.

The rest of them stayed awake with me, far into the night. Nan fell asleep sitting upright, her cheek against the wall. Pa stirred the fire, then pushed my chair closer. "Need anything, ma'am?" he said softly to Mrs. Smithson.

Mrs. Smithson shook her head. "Go on to sleep," she said to him. "I'll wake you, should I have need."

"I'll stay up with her," Hezzy said softly. "I did before."

"We can all stay up," Pa said. "Here we are."

My breath sounded harsh and loud. The fire crackled softly. The windows glowed from the moonlight outside. Slowly, without ever being aware of it, I slept too.

In the morning I still lived. Mrs. Smithson sent Nan on a round through the neighborhood, and more and more of our neighbors came. They sang hymns. The rasping of my breath sounded like an accompaniment. I could barely stop the work of breathing long enough to swallow the broth they made.

CHAPTER TWENTY-SEVEN

The morning of the second day, I reached what felt like the end. The work of breathing seemed not worth the effort it took. The crowded cabin faded from my sight. My mother sat with me, holding my hand.

The door of the cabin creaked open. I heard the rustle of silks and smelled lavender. "Miss Hannah," Miss Sarah said, "what has happened to our dear Elizabeth?"

Ma murmured something in reply. Mrs. Farah must have moved away from the fire, because Miss Sarah knelt beside me, her skirts brushing mine. She pulled me forward, onto her shoulder. For the barest moment I relaxed, but then my body seemed to seize.

"At first we thought she was sick like you," Ma said gently. "But you see—'tis not the same."

"Asthma." Hezzy's voice seemed to float across the room. I could not see Hezzy. "'Tis her asthma again."

"Yes," Miss Sarah said. "I heard from Ma Silver, and from Nan. I brought something Cook said might help. I bought it in Jonesborough. Have you tried camphor?"

I could not hear Ma's reply. A few minutes later someone put a wooden bowl onto my lap, full of steaming hot water and a sharp-smelling piney oil. Ma draped a dishcloth over my head, trapping me in a cloud of steam.

"There, Elizabeth," came a soothing voice. "Does that not feel better?"

It did not feel better. It did not feel worse. Perhaps it did help, for the next morning I still lived.

THEY TREATED ME with camphor again, twice more. Sometime after dinner I began to revive. My head cleared enough that I could look around the cabin again and notice who was there. Miss Sarah had spent the night and shared our fire with Mrs. Farah and Mrs. Cole.

The other women had never been friendly toward

Miss Sarah. Always before, if they happened to meet, they bristled like dogs do when they do not know each other. But now they talked quietly together, discussing my illness.

"There is not much lung sickness in Charleston," Miss Sarah said. "We have smallpox and flux, especially in summer, and much malaria, of course, but not so much sickness of the lungs. Some say the sea air is healing."

Hezzy had been stirring the fire. She sat down on the bench and looked wearily at Miss Sarah. "How?" she asked.

"How what, dear?" Miss Sarah wiped some soot from Hezzy's chin.

"How does the sea air heal lungs?"

Miss Sarah shook her head. "I could not tell you, Hezzy. In the summer when the heat is so bad, the air near Charleston feels like a smothering blanket. But whenever there is any wind at all, it blows in from the sea. The air smells like salt, clean and pure. I don't know if it truly can heal."

I was able to sleep then, for a few hours. I woke coughing, fighting for air. I felt as though my lungs were being squeezed together. Ma pounded my back until I coughed up phlegm, Mrs. Farah made tansy tea, and Miss Sarah prepared another camphor treatment. "Lizzy, Lizzy," Nan said, stroking my shoulder while I bent over the steaming bowl. "Aye, Nan," I whispered. 'Twas the first I'd spoken in two days. Nan's hand paused a moment, then rubbed my shoulder again more firmly.

On the fourth day my chest felt easier. By evening I felt I might live. By the next morning my family thought I might, and one by one our neighbors went home. Three days later I could breathe without pain.

I lived. I held Patsy again, and wiped the supper dishes, and sang to the tunes Hezzy played on her fife.

But some of the happiness was gone from our house. My family hovered around me. 'Twas as though they had doubted I would die but now did not. Pa grew quieter and more solemn. Hezzy rarely laughed, and Nan did not smile. Sometimes Ma's face trembled when she looked at me.

I was not afraid, but I could not do anything to help them.

CHAPTER TWENTY-EIGHT

Days passed, and then weeks. Spring scented the air. Pale green leaves appeared among the low shrubs on the hills. Most days I felt well enough, though now and again a sudden cold spell, or a run down a hillside, would make my lungs tighten again as if in a vise. "Tetchy," Ma Silver said. "Your lungs is tetchy, that's what." She gave me bitter teas and I drank them.

I understood that I did not have much time. Autumn would come quickly, and my sickness might come more quickly still. Ma had finished warping the loom for me, and it stood ready. "Nan," I said one chilly morning, "Hezzy, I shall need your help." I brought out the wool I had prepared so far, soft colors, yellow and green. I spread the bit of paper, where so long ago Hezzy had drawn her new coverlet pattern, on the table. Hezzy's eyes opened wide.

"I thought that lost, or used to start the fire," she said.

"Nay," said I, "I kept it safe. But I need your help, sister. You weave better than I do. Will you start it for me?"

Hezzy opened her mouth, then shut it.

" 'Twas your own to make," Nan protested. "Your one own thing, was what you called it."

"Now I would rather it were ours together," I said. "Will you spin for me, Nan? There is just a bit more wool. I will fill the bobbins, and once Hezzy has begun she can show me how to go on."

"Aye, then," Hezzy said briskly. She smiled seldom these days, and did not smile now. She hoisted herself onto the seat of the loom and began to fuss with the heddles. "I do not need that paper," she said to me. "I have it all in my head."

THE NEXT DAY Mr. William came visiting Hezzy. They sat on the step in the sunshine, and Hezzy played her flute for him. He took it from her and showed her a new tune. I came out of the cabin and squeezed myself between them. Hezzy elbowed me, but I ignored her.

"Mr. William," I said sweetly, making my voice as soft and childlike as possible, "I have a problem, and I pray ye to help me." I looked up at him wide-eyed. Sure enough, he pulled himself up proudly.

"Certainly, Miss Lizzy," he said. "I am always at your service."

"Hezzy is supposed to teach me to read," I said. "Since the baby is so much work, Ma says Hezzy has to school me."

Hezzy made a little noise and elbowed me again, harder. Mr. William looked surprised. "*Hezzy* teaches you?" he asked. "But I thought—"

Hezzy turned to him. "Thought what?" she said sharply.

Mr. William shook his head and smiled gently. "Nothing," he said. "Nothing of importance."

I looked at Mr. William beseechingly. "She is not a patient teacher," I said. "I am dreadful slow to learn, and she scolds me so."

"I do not!" Hezzy burst out. "Lizzy, for shame! Quit telling such stories!"

"I am pained to hear it," Mr. William said to me, as though Hezzy had not spoken. "But how can I help you, little Miss Lizzy? Shall I tell Hezzy not to scold?"

"No, sir," I said. "Could you teach me to read?"

Mr. William looked at Hezzy. She looked away,

blushing furiously. "Of certain," he said. "At least, we can begin. You know that we may not have much time."

I bit my lip. I had not realized that even Mr. William was watching for me to die. But his next words were, "We may be able to make some progress. I doubt I am leaving for Charleston for a few weeks, at least."

Hezzy turned back to him. "A few weeks! Are you truly going so soon?"

He smiled. " 'Tis longer than we intended to stay." He picked up Hezzy's flute and handed it to her. "I wish it were longer," he said quietly. "In truth, I shall be sorry not to see you."

"Will you teach me now?" I asked him. Hezzy glared at me. Mr. William, laughing, got up.

"Aye, Miss Persistence!" he said. "Find a stick and some good soft dirt. Miss Hezzy, have a care to watch us, and see if my tutoring be better than yours."

Mr. William drew some letters in the dirt for me.

" 'Tis all there are?" I asked, kneeling down to look at them.

"Well—no, 'tis merely a start," he said. He put the stick down. "There are twenty-six letters, Lizzy, do you know that?"

I shook my head.

"Here," Mr. William said patiently. "First let me draw them all."

He made two kinds of each letter, large and small, in the dirt. He stepped back from them. "Do you know any of them?" he asked.

I shook my head again. "I am so slow—" I began. Mr. William stopped me with a motion of his hand.

"You are not slow, Lizzy," he said. "Don't think that. I will tell you the names of the letters, and you will say them after me." So he did, over and over until I knew the letters by heart. Once or twice he glanced at Hezzy, to see if she was watching too.

" 'Twill be enough for now," he said at last. "See, Lizzy? You are not so slow."

"No, sir," I agreed. I smiled at him. "Not when you are so patient and kind."

Mr. William grinned. "Different from Miss Hezzy, am I?"

"Aye, sir," I said.

WHEN HE LEFT, Hezzy flew into a fury. "You should not have done that! Lizzy, how could you!" She swished her skirts and stamped her feet. "I was never so ashamed!"

I laughed. "Sister, I did it only for you. He'll not guess the truth. He doesn't pay me that much attention."

Hezzy's cheeks flamed. "He must know none of us

can read," she said. "Did you see how he looked at me? He must have guessed. Or Daniel told him—or he heard about our letter." She stamped her feet and repeated, "I was never so ashamed!"

I crouched in the dirt and studied Mr. William's alphabet. "If he knows, he hid it well," I said. "You should not be ashamed, Hezzy. Mr. William does not wish to shame you."

Hezzy snorted and whirled away. I sprang up after her. "Next," I said, "I'll ask him to spell out our names."

THE NEXT TIME Mr. William came visiting, he brought paper, a quill pen, and a bottle of ink. "You must not only read, Miss Lizzy, you must write as well," he said.

I had been working at the loom, but I got up and sat at the table. Hezzy took my place. The *clack* and *thump* of her weaving filled the cabin.

The quill felt clumsy in my hand. 'Twas so much larger than a needle. Mr. William sat beside me. After watching me struggle for a few minutes, he put his hand over mine to guide it. Together we wrote the alphabet in large, ink-spotted letters.

"There," said Mr. William. "Now you may study even when it rains. Practice writing, too, Lizzy. You will need to practice."

At the end of the paper he wrote our names for me, Lizzy, Hezzy, Patsy, and Nan. That was the second lesson.

MANY DAYS PASSED before he could come again. Miss Sarah visited and repeated what Mr. William had said, that they were leaving soon. When she said this, Hezzy looked away.

Miss Sarah put her hand to Hezzy's chin. "Will you miss us, then?"

"Oh, aye," Hezzy said, in as carefree a voice as she could manage. "Look, I have finished my pocket." She took it out from the basket where she kept it, and unfolded it for Miss Sarah to see.

Miss Sarah smiled. " 'Tis beautiful, Hezzy! A credit to your talents as a gentlewoman. But why aren't you wearing it now?"

Ma gave Hezzy's arm an affectionate squeeze. "She'll save it for her courting days," she said.

"Of course," Miss Sarah said. "And she has plenty of time yet before she needs to think of such things. But you'll look lovely, Hezzy, when you do." For several minutes Miss Sarah's gaze rested on Hezzy with a most peculiar expression. Soon she took her leave.

CHAPTER TWENTY-NINE

Three days later Miss Sarah returned. We were expecting the Smithsons, and I was watching for them, when I saw Miss Sarah marching firmly across our pasture, Mr. William trailing more slowly in her wake. I pulled back into the cabin. "Ma," I said, "Miss Sarah's coming."

Ma looked up from nursing Patsy. "Likely she has come to say good-bye."

"I wish she weren't going," Hezzy said.

Nan giggled. "You wish Mr. William weren't going," she said.

"Both of them," admitted Hezzy.

"She wants something," I said. "Miss Sarah does. You can tell by the way she's walking."

Ma smiled. "What could she want that we could give?"

Miss Sarah came in without knocking. She went straight to Ma's chair and knelt beside her, not as though begging but in the manner of a close friend. "Hannah," she said, "let me take Hezzy to Charleston."

Across the room, Hezzy gasped. She stood up from the loom. Her face slowly went white, and two spots of red appeared on her cheeks.

"Why, Sarah!" said Ma.

"I would raise her as my own," Miss Sarah said. "I have no daughters, you have four. Let me take Hezzy. I promise I will pay her passage back, any time she wishes to return. I will educate her as a lady. I can show her so many things. Hezzy—" She turned around toward my sister. "Hezzy, don't you want to go?"

We all of us stood frozen. Hezzy's chest heaved. She opened and shut her mouth. Mr. William came to the door, and Hezzy looked across the room at him.

"Hezzy?" Miss Sarah asked.

"No," said Hezzy. The word came out slowly, as though dragged from her mouth. She stared at Mr.

William for a moment, then looked at the ground. "Not me," she said softly. "Take Lizzy instead."

I gasped in turn. Hezzy turned and caught my eye. We looked at each other for a long moment, until I bowed my head.

"But Hezzy," Miss Sarah said gently, "I thought that you would love to go."

Hezzy *would* love to go. Hezzy would love to wear silk dresses and walk along the sea. To be an educated lady. To drink English tea.

"I would," Hezzy said. "Oh, I would! Thank you, Miss Sarah, thank you so much for wanting me. But take Lizzy, take her, please."

Miss Sarah looked at Ma and at me. Slowly she said to Hezzy, "Because the sea air may be healing, is that why?"

Hezzy nodded. Tears came to her eyes. A giant lump formed in my throat; I could not swallow.

"Aye," Hezzy said.

Miss Sarah shook her head. "Hezzy—Hannah—it may be healing, or it may not be. No one can say. Your sister is sickly, Hezzy. You would not wish her to die so far from home?"

Hezzy whispered, "I would not wish her to die at all."

Ma made a soft noise in her throat. She handed Patsy to Nan and tightened the front of her shift. Then she took Patsy back. "Find your pa," she said to Nan. "Bring him here." She smiled at Miss Sarah. It looked as though the smile pained her. "I could let Hezzy go, if her pa approves. But Lizzy—"

"No!" Hezzy said. "I will not go. Lizzy shall."

Miss Sarah spread her hands helplessly. "I should be glad to have Lizzy—I would have her with joy. But we must be clear about the danger. There are doctors in Charleston, we would do all we could. But I cannot guarantee her safety."

"You cannot guarantee Hezzy's safety," Ma said, a bit sharply.

"No," Miss Sarah admitted. She looked at me and for the first time spoke to me. "Lizzy, my dear, do you want to?"

You can be afraid of everything, or you can be afraid of nothing at all.

Truly I had been prepared to die, but to my surprise I was not fully prepared to live. I looked at tiny Patsy on my mother's lap, and Hezzy, so straight-backed and defiant. I thought of Nan and Pa. I expected to die among them. I was not prepared to be away from them. I did not want to go.

And yet I did. I felt as though I were stepping into a dark pit and could not see the bottom, but I knew that there must be a bottom somewhere. So I nodded, and held out my hands, and said, "Yes, please, Miss Sarah. Truly I would wish to go."

CHAPTER THIRTY

Pa and Nan were coming up the path. We could hear Nan's excited chattering. "We will talk it over and tell you our decision," Ma told Miss Sarah.

Miss Sarah bowed her head gracefully. "We leave tomorrow," she said. " 'Tis sudden, I know, but Mr. Beaumont has made plans."

Ma nodded. "Then we will send word soon."

Miss Sarah got up with a rustle of skirts. With one wistful look over her shoulder she went out the door. Mr. William, who had been standing by the wood box, stepped up to Ma and bowed low. "Good-bye, madam," he said formally. He took Hezzy's hand and bowed over it. "Good-bye, Miss Baker," he said.

" 'Tis not good-bye," Hezzy whispered. "Not yet."

Mr. William held her hand a moment longer, then

bowed silently to me and followed Miss Sarah. As he went out, Pa and Nan came in. Mr. William raised his hat to Pa. I looked out the window. Miss Sarah was already far across the field.

Pa rinsed his hands in the bucket by the door. Ma sat silently. We were all silent a moment, and then Hezzy and Nan spoke almost at once.

"She can't go!" said Nan.

Hezzy said, "She must!"

Pa raised his hand. He sat down heavily on the bench beside Ma. "Lizzy," he said, "come here. Do you want this fancy life?"

"No, Pa," I said. "But I want to go."

Pa wiped his face. "If we had somewhere else to send you . . . ," he began. "If the Beaumonts could see you safe to your folks back East—"

"There's none of them could take her," Ma said. "Haven't I thought of that? My pa could never care for a child. The rest, who knows where they be?"

"And they aren't on the sea," Hezzy said.

"The sea." Pa grunted. "Ye put a lot of faith in this sea, Hezzy."

"'Tis something to have faith in," she replied.

"Or ye could try God," he retorted sharply.

Nan crowded in, her face solemn and worried. "But the minister says God helps them that help themselves."

Pa looked unhappy. He turned to Ma. "'Twas only

Miss Sarah and young Mr. William who came?" Ma nodded. "That's not right," Pa said. "Mr. Beaumont ought to make the invitation, if he means it too. Lord, Lizzy, these folks is not like us. You'd be living with them, hear? You may not be wanting a fancy life, but you'd be getting one. Maybe you wouldn't like that. Maybe you wouldn't feel like yourself there."

"And they have slaves," said Nan.

"And they have slaves," Pa echoed. "And you could not speak out against that while you lived in their house."

"I would not have to speak out against it to be against it," I said.

Ma leaned forward and pushed my hair away from my face. "Lizzy, you are just a child."

"Ma," I said, "I am not afraid."

There was a sudden sharp knock on the door. We looked up, startled. Then Pa stood and smiled grimly. "Mr. Beaumont," he said, "please come in."

PA MOTIONED to the chair, but Mr. Beaumont swept the tails of his coat aside and took the bench by the hearth. "Sir," he said to Pa, "I meant to allow my wife to speak first. You should know that both of us would be grateful indeed to have Elizabeth entrusted to our care."

"Why?" Pa asked bluntly. "What would fine folk like yourselves want with our Lizzy? I'd not have her go to be a servant."

Mr. Beaumont looked distressed. "Indeed not, sir!" he said. "We invite her to live as a guest of our family."

" 'Tis a lot of trouble, taking on a child," Ma said softly.

Mr. Beaumont shook his head. "A child is what my wife wants most," he said. "Having Lizzy with us would be a comfort to her. 'Tis a small enough thing to me. 'Tis something I can easily do. We can provide well for Lizzy. There are fine doctors in Charleston; she would have the best of care." He smiled at me. "And every sort of thing you could want, Lizzy, ribbons, sweets—"

"Letters," I said.

His smile deepened and became more real. "Letters," he agreed. "Books." Then he looked up at Hezzy, who had hardly moved from the side of the loom. "I heard that you would rather your sister go," he said to her. "But we would be happy to have you both."

For a brief moment hope flared up in Hezzy's eyes, but Ma made a stricken sound, almost a sob, and Hezzy's face went smooth. "Thank you, sir, but no," she said softly. "One of us is enough."

Again silence filled the cabin. A log in the fire broke and fell into pieces with a shower of sparks. Both Pa and Mr. Beaumont seemed to be waiting. Finally Pa sighed heavily. "The lass can go if she will," he said.

CHAPTER THIRTY-ONE

Pa kept the fire built up all night long. Ma cleaned his old leather satchel and packed it with my extra shift, my winter stockings and cloak, my short gown and my Sunday petticoat. Hezzy quickly made a housewife for me, and Ma tucked a needle, some pins, and some thread into its pockets. Ma looked around the cabin. "So many things you might need."

"Miss Sarah will see to it," Pa said.

"Aye." Ma looked through her skeins of worsted yarn and added some to my bag.

"Your coverlet's not finished," Nan said.

"We could finish it tonight," Hezzy said quietly.

"We couldn't," I said. We were almost through with the weaving, but the finishing work would take too much time. "I never meant it for me anyway. I wove it for Patsy. Finish it for her." I snuggled my face next to Patsy's tiny one. I had held her ever since Miss Sarah had left, except when Ma was nursing. I could not bear to let go of her.

Patsy patted her hand against my cheek and laughed. Her breath smelled of milk. My sweet sister, who would forget me so soon.

Nan leaned against me. "She'll not forget you," she said, as if she could read my thoughts. "I will not let her."

"Poor Patsy," I said. "Poor Hezzy. I am sorry, Hez—"

"Shut up!" Hezzy said. "We will *never* speak of that. None of us. Promise me."

"I promise," I said softly. I cradled Patsy on my shoulder and reached for my alphabet paper, the one Mr. William and I had written. "You'll have to keep this," I told Hezzy. "Mr. William will help me make another. Someday I will write you all a letter. Mind, 'twill not be bad news."

"Someday," Hezzy said, her voice steady, "I will read it and write one back to you."

IN THE MORNING Hezzy tried to give me her red pocket, but I would not take it. Nan brought me

Sarah, my old doll. Pa hitched the horses to take us to the road where we would meet the Beaumonts and the stagecoach. Ma opened my satchel again and looked inside. "I put in the last of the apples," she said, closing it. "Something sweet for your journey."

We heard the creak of the wagon wheels as Pa brought the horses to the door. Hezzy started up, white-faced. Nan clutched my hand. I had to clear my throat twice before I could speak. "Can we—may we say good-bye here?" I whispered. "Here, while we are by ourselves alone?"

"We should see you as far as we can," Ma said. "Pa thought to follow the stage into Jonesborough."

"No, please," I whispered again. "I want to say good-bye now." I could not explain exactly why. I said, "Here while it's just us. Here at home."

So we kissed and hugged and I held Patsy one last small moment. "Oh, Nan," I said. "Oh, Ma." Then I climbed into the wagon next to Pa and he drove the two of us away. I did not look back.

Halfway to the stage road we heard footsteps running behind us. I turned, hoping it was not Hezzy, fearing to see her face. 'Twas Suzy Pearlette. Pa stopped the wagon and I leaned over the edge. "I just heard," she said, clutching my hand. "I'm glad to see you before you are gone." She pressed a small piece of cloth into my hand, a kerchief. "We none of us blame you for going," she said. "None of us do. But we'll miss you." Pa started the horses. "Good-bye!"

CHAPTER THIRTY-TWO

"We follow the Great Valley Road, then turn off toward Richmond," Miss Sarah said. "From Richmond we go by stage to Norfolk, and then we sail south to Charleston."

The coach jolted and bounced. 'Twas worse than a wagon. We were not halfway to Jonesborough, and already I felt shaken to pieces. Miss Sarah, Cook, and I shared the seat riding forward—the best seat, Miss Sarah said. A gentleman bound for Abingdon had the seat riding backward. The middle seat—nothing but a bench, really, without a back to it—was empty for now. Daniel was riding on top, and somewhere behind us Mr. Beaumont and Mr. William followed on horseback. Behind them, farther back, Pa was driving home from the little public house where we had met the Beaumonts. Or else he was home by now, currying the horses, smelling the bread Ma was baking. . . .

I shook my head. I would not think of it. "Lizzy, dear?" Miss Sarah asked. "Are you hearing me at all?"

I thought hard, then remembered what she had said. "Aye. The Great Valley Road—'twas how we came from Pennsylvania. Richmond, Norfolk, a boat to Charleston." I thought about this. "Why a boat? Why not take the stage the whole way?"

The coach hit a rock at good speed and careened sideways. Miss Sarah grabbed the window frame. I slid halfway onto Cook's lap.

"There are mountains in the way of the direct route," Miss Sarah said. "A man might cross on foot, perhaps, but we could not. Also there are hostile Indians, and swamplands. This way is easier. You'll like being on a ship, I'm sure. But that portion of our journey will not take long. Are you happy, dear Lizzy?"

"Not yet," I said. I looked out the window of the coach. My family was already out of sight, our farm gone. I felt lost, and we were not even to Jones-borough yet.

"You will be lonesome, I know," Miss Sarah said. Her fingers lightly brushed my forehead. "But you will be happy, too. I promise."

When we reached Jonesborough the coach stopped. Mr. Beaumont and Mr. William watered their horses and rested them, but Miss Sarah hurried me into one of the shops. She bought a small trunk and began to choose a flurry of other things, shoes and linens and broadcloth, an ivory hairbrush and a handful of ribbons. "Show the man your foot," she said. I realized with a shock that she was buying me shoes, that all these things were for me. "The trunk will keep your leather bag clean on the journey," she added carefully, watching my expression. "The rest are things you will need."

"I have shoes already," I said.

" 'Twill be good to have a spare pair, for the journey. We will not see many towns this size."

"I do not need these things," I said.

"Lizzy." Miss Sarah pulled me aside and spoke gently. "Here you dress as everyone here dresses. In Charleston I would like you to be dressed as everyone there dresses." She put her hand to my face. "Your mother would understand."

I hoped she would, for I could see little I could do about it. For a moment I thought of Hezzy, how this would delight her. I looked at the bolts of cloth laid out on the counter. The storekeeper was cutting bleached linen. Next was an indigo cotton. "Miss Sarah," I said. "I don't like to wear blue."

She frowned. "You don't? 'Twould look well on you."

"I should like a green dress," I offered. "Light green, like the one you have."

Miss Sarah smiled. "Of course," she said. "I should have asked you what you would prefer." She put the indigo cloth aside and helped me choose a sprigged green, then a wine-colored wool and a brown linsey. "White dresses are most fashionable," she said. "You shall have them in Charleston, but not, I think, while we travel by coach."

We went to the inn and ate a quick meal before the stage moved on. Mr. Beaumont raised his eyebrow at his wife. "Did it go well?" he asked.

Miss Sarah smiled at me. "Elizabeth has nice tastes," she said.

Before we left I put my satchel into my new trunk. Before I did that, I took my doll, Sarah, out. I held her on my lap through the next stage.

'Twas a fine bright day for travel. The far-off mountains came clearer and looked soft and green and inviting. Fine dust floated in through the open windows of the stagecoach. Three men shared the backward seat now. One of them must have greased his hair, because as the day wore on the dust settled onto the grease until his head looked like a patch of newly dug earth. I had trouble not to smile.

At night we stopped at a tavern. Miss Sarah and I shared a bed in a private room, and Cook slept next to it on the floor. Mr. Beaumont, Mr. William, and Daniel were somewhere else, I knew not where.

The bed ropes were loose and the bed sagged. I felt I had to hold myself tight to keep from rolling onto Miss Sarah. The air smelled strange and the pillow musty. The mutton we had eaten at supper churned inside my stomach. I tried not to think of home.

After a time, a sliver of moonlight shone through a crack of the shuttered window. I was not crying, but neither was I near to sleep. I looked over the edge of the bed, and saw Cook also lying wide awake in the quiet room. When she saw me looking at her, she slowly closed her eyes.

In the morning I asked, "Why couldn't you sleep last night?"

She gave me a blank look. "I slept fine, miss, just fine."

"No, I saw you awake."

"No, miss. I slept fine."

"Is something the matter, Cook?" Miss Sarah asked.

"No, ma'am, I slept fine."

I saw then that I should not have persisted. I could cause trouble where I meant none. When Miss Sarah had gone down to breakfast I said, "I'm sorry, Cook. I didn't think."

Cook shook her head. "Nothing to be sorry about. I slept fine."

"Your name isn't Cook, is it?" I asked.

She gave me a look that might have contained a glimmer of a smile. "You call me Cook, miss. That'll be all right."

Before we set out again I searched through my satchel for the apples Ma had sent. In the very bottom, beneath my folded clothes, I found my carders, a big piece of well-washed wool, and our best drop spindle too. I pulled them out and held them, and tears rolled down my cheeks.

'TWAS IMPOSSIBLE to sew inside a bouncing coach, but I could spin there.

The first night Cook had measured me and cut the fabric Miss Sarah had bought. After that, every night if we had time, all three of us sewed my new clothes. By the time we were halfway to Richmond I had a dress styled like Miss Sarah's, which Miss Sarah called a chemise, and a shift with ruffled sleeves and a neckline to match the dress. I looked as if I belonged with the Beaumonts. I understood that I should not wear my old clothes again.

Yet the Beaumonts did not seek to shame me. They spoke well of my family and of me. Miss Sarah did not buy me a new doll or ask me to put mine away. Even Mr. Beaumont still seemed pleased to have me with them; he was sometimes alarming, but never cross.

And all day long, in the jolting coach, they smiled at me while I spun. I was determined to make my wool last as long as possible, so I spun thread as fine as a spider's web. "I never dreamed you were so talented, Elizabeth," Miss Sarah said. They all called me Elizabeth now. "In Charleston you can knit yourself an evening shawl."

William continued to teach me in the evenings as well. He read Bible verses to me and made me read them back to him. Soon the words began to make sense. As we bounced closer to my new home, to Charleston, I began to plan what I would write to Hezzy.

EPILOGUE

NORFOLK, VIRGINIA
1 AUGUST 1792

Dear Sisters Hezzy, and Nan, and Patsy,
and Most Loving Mother and Father,

I send you this from Norfolk. Thus far we have com-
pleted our journey in good health, all of us well. The
Beaumonts treat me with kindness, except for William,
who treats me as a younger sister, someone to tease and
annoy. Only, Hezzy, he is a patient teacher. He is helping
me spell now, and he says if I can write this letter out with
no blots or grave errors, he will give me an ink bottle of my
own.

I told him I would rather have a fleece. I have been homesick often but the morning I found the spindle is the only time I have cried. I have spun all the wool now and must wait until Charleston to get more, as we have not time to shop for such things here. Mr. Beaumont says we may be able to add some sheep to the plantation.

The ocean looks like a great green griddlecake, flat but as wide as the sky. William says it does not feel flat when you sail on it. I will have to wait until tomorrow to see if that is true.

Miss Sarah suggests I call her "Aunt Sarah" and Mr. Beaumont "Uncle William." I hope you will not mind.

The air does seem different here. It smells of salt and when I breathe, it seems to go all the way down to the bottom of my lungs. 'Tis an easy feeling. Nan, you must know, I will not be wearing indigo. When next you see Ma Silver, tell her this: I am still not afraid.

Your ever loving,
Lizzy

Author's Note

The first questions everyone asks me about *Weaver's Daughter* are "What's really wrong with Lizzy? And will the sea air cure her?"

I did a lot of research about eighteenth-century American life before I wrote this book, but I did not need to research the details of Lizzy's illness. Like Lizzy, I have asthma, and I gave her my own medical history—without the modern treatments that have let me live a normal life.

Asthma is a disease in which the passageways of the lungs become irritated and stiff. People with asthma don't have trouble breathing in, though they often feel as if they do. They have trouble breathing *out,* and since they can't easily get rid of the old air in their lungs, they can't easily breathe in new air. People suffering from asthma make wheezing sounds when they breathe, and they cough because of the mucus caught in their lungs.

Even now, asthma kills people. I once suffered a sudden,

severe attack while galloping my horse across country, a mile from any road. I lost consciousness. It took months—and lots of medicine—before my lungs returned to normal. (It was also the last time I rode across country without my emergency medicine in my pocket!) Asthma can kill people suddenly, in an acute attack, but it can also kill slowly, as it almost kills Lizzy in my story.

Most of the time, people who have asthma can keep it under control. My doctor likens asthma to a smoldering fire that flares up only when you throw more fuel onto it. Sudden exposure to cold air; sudden, vigorous exercise; any sort of virus or cold; and, especially, any sort of allergic reaction can trigger asthma. Lizzy, like me, has severe seasonal allergies that make her asthma especially bad in the fall—until the first frost kills the plants that she's allergic to.

Asthma is more common now than ever before—doctors are not sure why—but it was known and documented in Lizzy's time. Medicine was in its infancy then. In fact, people who could afford doctors died more quickly than people who could not, because the doctors' treatments sometimes made people worse. For the most part, the doctors of the time were doing the best they could, with very little actual knowledge. They could see and record symptoms, but they had no idea what was causing them. In the eighteenth century no one knew that bacteria and viruses caused disease, so doctors rarely washed their hands, let alone their equipment. Eighteenth-century doctors had no X rays, no anesthesia, no medical tests of any sort. They had very little way of knowing what went on inside the human body.

So doctors like the one in my book often clung to old

theories. They believed that the body contained four different substances called humours—blood, phlegm, black bile, and yellow bile—and that for a person to be healthy these humours had to be kept in balance. When the doctor in my book makes Lizzy vomit again and again, he is trying to get rid of her extra phlegm—the snot and mucus caused by her allergies. Making her throw up would help her if she had been poisoned, but it did nothing at all for her asthma and allergies, and probably made her weaker and sicker.

Ma Silver, unlike the doctor, does not guess at the cause of Lizzy's illness. Instead she treats Lizzy's symptoms—her wheezing, congestion, and irritated eyes—with herbal remedies, homemade treatments made from plants. Ma Silver—and later Miss Sarah, with the camphor—brings Lizzy some relief. Many herbs contain medicines.

But Ma Silver's herbs don't treat Lizzy's underlying illness, her asthma. And Lizzy can't avoid plant pollen, as I do today, by sitting in an air-conditioned room. But she does move to South Carolina with the Beaumonts. Will it help?

Maybe. People with allergies are allergic to specific plants, not to all plants, and different plants grow in different parts of the country. I have lived in Indiana, Massachusetts, and Tennessee; my allergies were bad in Indiana, were moderate in Massachusetts, and are really awful in Tennessee. But last year, as I was beginning *Weaver's Daughter* at the height of a bad allergy season, I went for a week to the Carolina coast. The wind blew in strongly from the sea, across salt marshes, and I breathed easily the whole time I was there.

Lizzy could still get a bad cold in Charleston that would trigger a severe attack of her asthma. She could still die. But living in Charleston should help her.

Usually when I research history I study newspapers, letters, photographs, and other documents from the period. But this book takes place in 1791 and 1792. Cameras hadn't been invented yet, there are no surviving newspapers from my corner of the Southwest Territory, and very few surviving documents relate to the common life Lizzy and her family led. Luckily I live just down the road from the Rocky Mount Museum, in Piney Flats, Tennessee. In 1770 a man named William Cobb built a house there that still stands and is now the heart of the museum. For the dedicated staff at Rocky Mount, every year is 1791, the year the newly appointed governor of the newly created Southwest Territory, William Blount, lived with the Cobbs and ran the territory from Rocky Mount.

The people who work at Rocky Mount now portray the Cobbs, various government officials, and other historical figures as they would have lived then. Rocky Mount has a wonderful library of original source material, which they let me read and study. They also allowed me to become Hannah Baker, the weaver, Lizzy's mother, with her dress, her history, and, in time, her way of speaking.

Once I felt I knew Lizzy's mother well, I could easily imagine Lizzy and her sisters, and the life they led without cars, computers, clocks, or books.

About the Author

Kimberly Brubaker Bradley was born in Fort Wayne, Indiana. After earning her bachelor's degree from Smith College, she worked as a research chemist, then became a freelance writer. Her first novel, *Ruthie's Gift,* won her a *Publishers Weekly* "Flying Start" honor. Its companion, *One-of-a-Kind Mallie,* was praised by *Kirkus Reviews* as "a warm, loving story." Kimberly Brubaker Bradley and her husband, Bart, have two young children, Matthew and Katie. They live in eastern Tennessee, in the foothills of the Appalachian Mountains.